I0608444

DREAMING OF TOMORROW

Susan Kohler

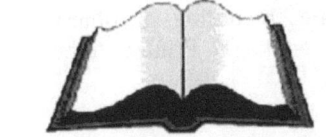

CCB Publishing
British Columbia, Canada

Dreaming of Tomorrow

Copyright ©2011 by Susan Kohler
ISBN-13   978-1-926918-72-3
First Edition

Library and Archives Canada Cataloguing in Publication
Kohler, Susan, 1950-
Dreaming of tomorrow / written by Susan Kohler – 1st ed.
ISBN 978-1-926918-72-3
Also available in electronic format.
I. Title.
PS3611.O47D74 2011   813'.6   C2011-905420-5

Original cover art design by Jinger Heaston: www.jingraphix.org

The characters and events in this book are fictitious unless otherwise noted by the author. Any similarity to real persons, living or dead, is coincidental and not intended by the author.

Extreme care has been taken to ensure that all information presented in this book is accurate and up to date at the time of publishing. Neither the author nor the publisher can be held responsible for any errors or omissions. Additionally, neither is any liability assumed for damages resulting from the use of the information contained herein.

All rights reserved. No part of this publication may be reproduced, stored in a retrieval system or transmitted in any form or by any means, electronic, mechanical, photocopying, recording or otherwise without the express written permission of the publisher. Printed in the United States of America and the United Kingdom.

Publisher: CCB Publishing
British Columbia, Canada
www.ccbpublishing.com

Dedication

To Martha Roper and Josie's Target,
the best horse and rider team I ever knew.

Author's Note

This is the third book I've written using Kate and Laura as the matchmakers, so some of the characters have appeared in one of my other novels.

This one is different, though. This is partly autobiographical, without the hunky hero. (darn!) The stories about Mae really happened to my mother, Iona Mae Kohler. My father lost his battle with cancer. Please don't think this is a sad story though, it's like life: happy, sad, and funny, sometimes all at once.

When I had this almost half finished, I had the idea to put more of my personal faith into this book. I checked the guidelines for Christian romance novels and I respected them, but I decided not to change what I had written to conform to those guidelines. I believe that not every Christian is perfect; they have human frailties, needs and desires. Even good Christians can feel passion.

To me, the trick is how you use those feelings and what's in your heart. So if you think this book is too preachy, please try to understand; if you feel this book is too sexy, please forgive me.

The way I see it, if half of you think it's too preachy and half of you think it's too sexy, I've hit my goal.

Sue

Prologue

Emily Ralston was a dreamer. She had always had a good life, but lately her life had become painful and complicated, so she filled her spare time dreaming of a simple life, when she could focus on herself instead of her family. She would finish school, lose weight, get a great job, and maybe--just maybe meet a wonderful man and get married.

Part of her hoped that simple life would never really come. In fact, she dreaded it. To get to that easier, simple life she would have to lose almost everything and everyone she loved. The future, aside from her dreams, terrified her.

The thing Emily had forgotten, was God doesn't always follow your plans and dreams.

He has His own plans for your life, and they can be wonderful.

And He doesn't always wait until you think the time is right.

Chapter One

Emily Ralston stood in the hot sun holding the strong, wooden gate wide open, nursing a raging headache and wondering how she'd gotten herself into this mess. She was hot, covered with dust and dirt, and very sweaty. She was also afraid, but she felt too shy to ask for help. Her throat was so dry she felt like a gold miner in an old movie, wandering around in a barren desert, just before he fell silently to the sand. She had a bitter, thick taste in her mouth. She was also uncomfortable in her stiff new jeans, her feet hurt, and she had a throbbing splinter in her thumb.

It was only the second event of the horse show. She should have known she would get herself into trouble the minute she went along with one of Laura's crazy schemes. Laura Kelsey, who was very far along in her first pregnancy, had persuaded Emily to volunteer to help out at the riding club's annual charity horse show while she stayed home and took care of Emily's ailing parents.

She watched the horse and rider running in the arena vaguely, with an amateur's eyes. The action in the arena meant less than nothing to her. She didn't know anyone there, had no knowledge of horses or horse shows, and she was not coping very well with her first introduction to them. The horses were large beasts, hairy, smelly and covered with sweat. They left muddy spots of smelly urine and the huge piles of smelly manure on the ground behind them was even worse! It drew flies by the dozens. It was hard to avoid stepping in some of it, sooner or later. Sooner in Emily's case.

Not only that, but some of the gigantic beasts pitched a fit before going into the arena. They terrified Emily. Even worse, some of the them acted as if they were going to smash through the fence coming out. And, to top it off, one of the great beasts had sneezed on her! Yuck!

Emily decided she was going to kill Laura when she got home. Just because Laura was eight months pregnant she thought it would be too hard on her to work all day at the charity horse show. Ha! She was probably even lying about having a difficult pregnancy just so she could convince Emily to come help out at the show in her place. Emily thought back once again to the conversation she had with Laura.

Laura had made it sound like helping out at the horse show would be fun, selling Emily on the idea of taking a day off from the grinding routine of dealing with her father's terminal cancer and her mother, who was in the early stages of senile dementia. She pushed Emily to get out of the house and meet some new people. Laura stressed how nice the members of the riding club were. She pleaded that the dust and the unseasonable heat were too much for her at that stage of her pregnancy. She complained that there wasn't any place at the arena that was comfortable for her to sit and put her swollen feet up. She even laughed away Emily's protests that she didn't know anything about horses.

"They'll stick you in the food stand, or ask you to help out the announcer or the show secretary, something like that. You'll hardly even see a horse. I'll have Kate and her husband, Bob, watch out for you. Trust me." Laura conned her with a smile before continuing, "And you know that I'll take good care of your folks, I'll even get Jack to help me."

"Well. . ." Emily hesitated.

"Come on Emily, let's trade places, just for one day." Laura persuaded, "Jack and I will take care of your folks and you can help out at the charity show. It benefits the American Cancer Society."

"But I don't know anything about horses," Emily protested

weakly, "and I think I'm afraid of them."

"Chicken!" Laura teased in a gentle tone. "I'll take care of it. You won't even have to go near a horse. Do it Em, you might even meet a cute cowboy."

"Sure, and what cute cowboy would be interested in me?" Emily muttered.

"Stop it, Em," Laura snapped, her temper flaring. "I'll tell you what kind of cute cowboy would be interested in you, a smart one! One who could see what a really terrific person you are."

"Oh sure," Emily said, shaking her head sadly. "I'll keep an eye out for him."

"I'm sure you will," Laura said softly, "just so you can push him away."

"Laura," Emily was suddenly suspicious, "this business of me going to a horse show isn't just one of your famous set-ups, is it? You wouldn't dare do that to me, would, you?"

Laura was infamous for her skill and success at matchmaking.

"You know me, Emily." She grinned widely. "What do you think?"

"Never mind, it wouldn't work anyway." Emily smiled sadly as she went out the door. "I'll probably be your only failure."

Emily never knew that Laura had grinned at the closed door and stuck out her tongue before saying to the empty room, "Wanna bet?"

So the job trade had taken place. Laura, the riding club's show secretary, was taking care of her parents, and Emily was standing in the hot sun at the horse show, covered with dust, acting as a very unglorified doorman for rowdy gymkhana horses. Kate and her husband had not shown up because two of her children had come down with the flu. To top it off, the people who were in charge of the horse show ignored her protests that she didn't like horses or know anything about them and put her on duty at the arena gate.

"You can open and close a gate, can't you?" a harried woman

said, pointing Emily towards the arena.

Emily had learned several things about horse shows: to keep out of the way of the horses' hooves, to lean against the fence and pretend to watch the event, and most importantly she was to never, ever open the gate until she was sure the rider inside was ready to exit the arena. Emily had even learned a few new words, words she was sure she'd never use herself, words like: hoof pick, sweat scraper, and pole bending.

Emily was jerked back to the present when a horse stopped right in front of her, kicking up a small cloud of dust and dirt that showered over her. It caused her to blink her eyes and cough.

"Hey Ma'am," a male voice said with a subtle trace of amusement, "you gonna open that gate or do I have to make Target here jump over it?"

"Sorry." Emily nearly jumped as she looked up at the rider on the other side of the fence. He was grinning at her, a warm friendly grin and he was gorgeous. Emily was stunned.

"Of course I'll open it." A rare hint of humor crept into her voice as she returned the smile. "Unless you want to just pick up that horse there and toss him over it."

"No ma'am." The cowboy winked at her. "I think I'll just let you open the gate so I can go through the normal way, if it's all the same to you."

"As long as you're sure." Emily managed to sound doubtful as she opened the gate and let the rider out.

She watched him as he rode away, then waited until the next rider went in before closing the gate again.

Surprisingly, she was beginning to relax. Unfortunately the next horse shattered that tiny bit of calm because it shied from entering the arena. This was one of the recalcitrant horses, intent on backing away from the opening his rider was asking him to go through. He was causing a lot of trouble, bumping into other horses and upsetting them. He took one step in and pushed back. He pushed the gate against Emily, who was backed up against another fence, sandwiching her. Emily was terrified, afraid of being crushed to death on the spot, when suddenly the pressure on her eased as the cowboy swung off his horse and quickly worked his way in beside her, pushing hard on the gate and yelling at the horse and rider.

"Damn it, Mark!" he yelled at the horse's rider. "Get him off this gate before you scare this girl to death!"

"Sorry!" Mark yelled, kicking frantically.

Even as he kicked at the horse, two other men came behind the animal and locked arms behind the horse's massive hindquarters, while a third grabbed the reins and pointed the horse's head into the arena. Careful to avoid the animal's hooves, the men pushed the horse into the arena. As the horse moved forward the cowboy next to Emily began to shut the gate, keeping a pressure on the horse, so that the only open space for the animal was the actual arena.

Some of the other riders even got behind the horse and slapped his rump, clicking at him and at the same time avoiding the horse's hind hooves. They grabbed the reins and led the horse up to the edge of the gate. The longer all this went on, the more frightened Emily became. Due to the rules, they couldn't lead the horse all the way in, they had to stop at the gate and push the horse in. Taking her cue from the cowboy, Emily kept pushing the horse using the gate to goad the animal into the arena. Finally the horse was in and the gate shut behind him. When they finally got the horse in, Emily turned to the man who had helped her.

"Thank you. I'm really glad for your help," Emily said quietly, looking once again into the most handsome face she'd ever seen.

He was so good looking that Emily froze up the minute her eyes met his. Tall and trim with black hair and brilliant blue eyes, his face was filled with humor and a hint of the devil. Oh my God! Emily thought as she felt the pull of attraction, I guess my libido isn't completely dead. Her next thought was: Down girl, he's way too handsome for you, guys like that never even give you the time of day.

"It's nothing. You looked like you could use some help." He grinned back at her, feeling his own jolt of surprise. "Hey, you're really scared, aren't you? I guess you're not used to spooked horses."

The man smiled at her, but the smile didn't seem real somehow and his voice was stern as he asked, "You obviously don't know anything about horses. How did you wind up with gate duty?"

"My friend Laura convinced me to help out today. She said it was for charity. She also said it would be fun and that I wouldn't have to be close to any horses. I'm sorry if I'm not doing a good job," Emily dropped her eyes, "but I'm a little afraid of these horses, they're so unruly."

"That's not what I meant, you're doing fine. Don't judge all horses by these. These are gymkhana horses. Gymkhana is a timed sport, and these are fast, high-spirited horses. Sometimes they get excited when they know they're going to run. Also some of the riders are more concerned with speed than they are with their horse's manners, since there's no judge marking them on their form." He paused, picking his words carefully. "Contrary to how it seems, some of these horses are highly trained and they really enjoy what they do. Watch that horse now. You'll see that he's running on his own, and that he turns easily, with very little steering from his rider."

The horse they had fought so hard with to get into the ring was running around some tall poles. Even to Emily's novice eyes the ride was smooth and balanced. The horse seemed to be running at breakneck speed with very little urging from the teenage boy on his back. The horse came to a stop with a toss of his head and pranced over to the gate. Emily opened the gate and let him out of the arena.

"See? He enjoyed his run. His rowdy behavior before was a sort of stage fright, maybe an equine form of performance anxiety that was causing him to act up going in, but it was not fear. That prance you see now is pure equine pride, he thinks he's hot stuff. Hell, he knows it."

"It's the first time I've even seen horses outside of the movies," Emily explained. "And they're so big and intimidating, especially the bad-mannered ones."

The horse walked away from the arena calmly. Together, they held the gate open and let another horse and rider enter.

"See how calm he is now?" the cowboy asked.

Emily turned her head and watched the horse and rider as they walked over to a nearby horse trailer. "Yes."

"Some of those bad-mannered horses are just excited, it's like pre-game nerves for any athlete before they compete," the cowboy explained, before adding, "I'm David, by the way, David Silvan."

David shook hands with Emily, noting her shy smile and also noticing something more, a deep sadness in her eyes. A sadness her smile couldn't even begin to hide.

"I'm Emily Culver," she answered shyly, surprised at the attention. "I've noticed your horse doesn't act up like that. Your horse walks in quietly and then just sort of explodes through the course. Look at the way he's just standing there now. Shouldn't you tie him up or something?"

"Target's okay, he's well trained. It's the training and treating the horse right, along with the nature of the horse that makes most of the difference. Most horses are calm, even lazy, although some horses will always be high strung," David said. "Now answer a question for me: How did a non-horse lover like you wind up working the gate? That's usually a position reserved for someone who-"

"Knows what the heck they're doing?" Emily finished as David trailed off. "My friend, Laura, was supposed to volunteer to work at the show but she's very pregnant, so she offered to stay home with my folks while I came here. She said I wouldn't even have to see a horse. When I showed up someone asked if I could open and close the gate. It didn't sound too hard so I said yes."

"So here you are stuck out in the full heat of the sun, scared of the horses, thirsty and covered in dust." David grinned, "Helluva way to treat a volunteer."

"Excuse me, but I'm going to go find the idiot who put you out here on the gate and skin him alive." The icy edge was back in his smile as he continued, "It's just plain cruel to do that to someone who's afraid of horses. It's also dangerous, not only for you, because you don't know how to avoid getting hurt, but also for the riders because you don't know how to help them or even how to tell when they need help."

Chapter Two

"I don't want to be any trouble." Emily seemed panicked at the thought of drawing any attention to herself.

"Don't give it another thought. It's not just for you, it's also for safety." David yelled up at the announcer's stand, "Hey Mac! Find Cliff and get him over here quick!"

"Cliff to the In-gate! Cliff go to the In-gate please." Came over the speakers.

"What's the problem. David?" A middle aged man with a cowboy hat, a florid face and a belly hanging over his belt buckle soon came jogging over.

Just as Cliff came over, the event ended and there was a break in the action in the arena. David and Emily opened the gate wide so that all the riders could go in to get their awards. David stayed where he was, with Emily, and listened as the awards were announced. Most of the riders led their horses in to get their awards, but some rode. They gave out awards for all three age groups at once.

The twelve and under group surprised Emily, since some of their horses seemed almost asleep, and others were prancing energetically. Next came the thirteen to seventeen group. Most of them seemed to be typical teenagers, and their horses were just a bit crazy, with only a few that were calm and well-mannered. The seniors ran the gamut from sedate to frisky. While the riders got their awards, some men were busy in the arena moving tall poles around, measuring the distance between each one.

As the awards were given out David turned to Cliff.

"I want to know whose bone-headed idea it was to stick a woman on the gate who not only doesn't know a thing about horses, but is scared of them to boot! Not only that, but there's no chair here for her. To top it off, she's dying of thirst. Is that how we treat a volunteer?" He was livid. "It's stupid, and potentially dangerous, and it's a hell of a way to treat someone who's trying to help out."

"I'm sorry, Ma'am," Cliff said to Emily. "I can replace you on the gate, if you wish."

"Or I can help you until you get used to the job," David offered, "and give you some insights on what's going on with various horses and riders."

"I'd really like that David, but could you do that and still ride? I'd hate to cause any fuss," Emily said softly because she was enjoying his company.

"Sure I can. Target's no problem." He grinned at her. "I'll just get someone to walk him around and keep him loose until I need to ride again."

"In that case, I'll stay, with your help. I'm really not that afraid." Emily smiled at him.

Heck, it was one way to keep talking to the best looking man she'd ever seen. It was worth putting up with the horses just to spend some time with this thoughtful, friendly and gorgeous man. He couldn't possibly know how unaccustomed she was to any attention from a man. Spending time with any man, other than her father, was rare for her. David seemed so nice too. She knew it was hopeless, he'd never be really interested in her but it was nice to be around him for a while. Half an hour of innocent talk with him would feed her daydreams and secret fantasies for a year.

"Okay, I'll work alongside you and help you get the hang of it," David replied, looking into her soft brown eyes and noticing the eagerness in her expression. "But I'm still going to kick some butt, if you'll pardon the expression."

"I agree." Cliff turned to Emily. "I'm sorry Ma'am, if you want, I'll send someone out to relieve you as soon as possible."

"I'll be okay, I guess." She looked over at David and smiled shyly. "David here said he'd help me out."

"There's still the little matter of something to drink, and a chair." David squinted at Cliff. "Do me a favor and take Target to the trailer and ask Nikki to walk him around for me after the awards are handed out."

"I'll get right on it. And Ma'am, feel free to shout up at Rusty if you want to be replaced, this is a horse show not a slave labor camp." Cliff walked away only to return a few minutes later with a pair of cold beers. He handed one to Emily and one to David. "This is just a start, I'll be back with a cooler and a chair. Thanks again for helping us out, Ma'am, we surely do appreciate it."

"Thanks." Emily very seldom drank alcohol but she pulled the tab and gulped the ice cold beer.

She had forgotten to bring any cold drinks with her and it seemed like she was too busy to head up to the cook shack. David watched with amusement as she drained her beer in one long gulp, handing her his unopened beer as soon as hers was gone. There was something appealing about this girl, he decided. She was so determined to do this dirty little job, and enjoy it, in spite of her shyness and the haunting sadness that never left her eyes.

"Here, take this. I have lots of cold drinks in my motor home," he offered.

"Thanks." Emily grinned, took the can and drank the second beer more slowly.

She was so thirsty, she never noticed someone coming over and taking David's horse.

"Hey!" she exclaimed. "Where's your horse?"

"Cliff took him over to my trailer to get him out of the way. I'll ask Nikki to walk him around to keep him loose." David explained, "It can be dangerous for a horse to cool off too much between events or to run without being warmed up."

He looked up and saw Cliff hurrying back. "Here comes

11

Cliff with a chair and a cooler."

"Here you go Ma'am, I'm sorry that took so long." Cliff smiled at her as he opened up the folding chair.

"It's no problem, thank you, Cliff." Emily smiled. "I'm Emily, by the way."

"Nice to meet ya' Emily," Cliff drawled. "Regardless of how it looks, we appreciate our volunteers."

He tipped his cowboy hat and left.

David pulled open the cooler. "I hope you like beer. I should have known that's what Cliff would bring you."

He waited for her response, then as she nodded he pulled out two cans, opened one and handed it to her.

"Wow! That's three beers in one day. I almost never drink beer but today it seems perfect. Thank you." Emily accepted the can.

David opened the second can for himself.

"Here, David." A woman rode up, leading David's horse.

She handed him a silver plate, about 10 inches in diameter. "You looked busy so I grabbed it for you." Even dirty, with her hat pulled low to shield her face and sunglasses covering her eyes, Emily could tell she was gorgeous, and thin. Damn!

"Thanks, Nick," David said in an off-handed tone. "Hey! Thanks for taking care of Target for me. Will you walk him until you have to ride? And throw this thing in the trailer?"

He handed the trophy back to her.

"Sure thing." She walked her horse to David's trailer to take care of Target.

The show started up again. As they talked, David and Emily let horses in and out. He explained the event to her and pointed out which riders were the best and which were not. The first group of horses had very young riders.

"Now, you must know by now that these are timed events and they are divided into age groups, 12 and under, 13 to 17, 18 and over. There are time penalties for knocking over a pole or a barrel, and going off course is a disqualification. Did you notice anything different about this sport than other sports?" David asked.

"Well, the horses for one thing," Emily said, grinning. "It's like a team sport with an animal as a teammate."

"Exactly!" David smiled at her. "I approve of the way you put it. The best riders and horses really do form a team. What else?"

"Well, most sports have separate competitions for men and women," Emily mused.

"And we don't," David said. "We compete head to head. Sometimes there are separate events for men and women but usually there are just age groups. The third difference is more subtle: we cheer each other on. We'll cheer a good ride. We'll all run out to help if a rider falls. We loan each other equipment if something breaks. We even offer advice to help a new rider. Then we go all out to win. The sportsmanship you learn at these shows, if you have a brain, is excellent."

"If you have a brain?" Emily prompted.

"There's always one hot shot who just can't grasp the concept of sportsmanship, but for the most part the riders all support each other," David explained.

The announcer called for the 13 to 17 riders to get ready, giving the numbers of the next three to go: "All right heads up! Number 25 in the arena; number 28 on deck; 42 get ready and then we move to the 13 to 17 group, with number 53 going first."

"This event, if you didn't hear the announcer, is called Pole bending. The horses weave through the poles which are spaced twenty feet apart, and are timed. Watch that rider there." He pointed to the girl waiting to go into the arena. "She's the state champion for her age group in this event. Notice how she barely skims through the poles, without wasting any motion or losing her horse's forward momentum. She and her horse are so in tune with each other that you can hardly see her give him any signals."

Emily watched and saw that the girl and her horse did indeed move as a perfect team through the poles, which were about six feet tall and just over an inch in diameter, painted white, with round flat bases to hold them up, not too much bigger around than the poles themselves. She let the girl out and the next rider in.

"Now watch him, he's new to the sport, not as talented, but with potential. See the differences in his ride?" David watched with a critical eye. "I think he should slow down just a bit until he gets the horse more schooled."

Emily watched and realized that she could see exactly what David meant. The boy's ride was choppy and rough; he had to really work hard to get the horse around the course, and there was no flow, no rhythm to the ride. She told David that.

"Exactly!" David was proud of her insight.

"Watch this girl." He pointed out a slightly older rider. She had a very rough ride, knocked over two poles, and got a bad time. "She used to be really good."

"She didn't seem very good to me," Emily puzzled.

"She wasn't good today," David said in a disapproving tone. "That's what can happen when a teenage girl discovers boys and forgets to practice her horse."

"Why are so many of the horses male?" Emily asked.

For an answer he pointed out a horse over by a red trailer. Every few minutes the horse would squeal and kick out at nothing in particular.

"See that mare? She's in heat once a month."

"Even I don't that bitchy every month," Emily quipped.

"Thank God." David grinned as he reached out with one arm and gently squeezed her shoulder.

"Doesn't having a mare in heat arouse the male horses?" Emily asked.

"Most of these old boys are geldings," David grinned, "which means they don't have all their, umm, original equipment."

His running commentary made the show much more

interesting for Emily. He was a lively conversationalist, with a subtle sense of humor. Emily forgot her usual awkwardness around men, or more specifically a handsome man, and began to really enjoy herself.

The gorgeous woman rode up with David's horse.

"Will you be okay until I get back?" he asked before mounting the huge black horse.

"Sure, I'll be fine." Emily smiled at him. "Good luck."

David mounted and rode his horse over to the warm up arena. Emily watched him between opening and closing the gate. He looked great on a horse, natural and relaxed, but heck, Emily thought, he'd look great anywhere. The teenagers finished and the senior riders started through the course. David was second, right after the gorgeous woman. Someone came over to talk with Emily and she didn't catch the woman's name. She did notice the woman's ride however, it was one of the fastest of the day. Great! She looks terrific and she can ride like a demon!

David was next. His horse entered the arena looking lazy. Target was a giant, muscular horse, almost coal black. He trudged in, looking like he couldn't run if he tried. David sat relaxed and held the reins loosely in one hand. Target plodded calmly over to the starting point and stood still. David picked up the reins with both hands and made a clicking sound, and Target exploded into a burst of blinding speed. He wove through the poles as easy as it could be done, then after crossing the finish line he stopped, settled down and plodded slowly out of the arena. The announcer called out his time, and it was the best so far. The time held up after all the riders had run the poles, so David had won the senior event. This time he went in to accept the small sliver plate. He gave the plate to Emily as he left the arena.

"Here's a memento for helping us out today." He dismounted. "Let's go get something to drink before they begin the next event."

"I can't take this, you won it," Emily protested.

"I have plenty of 'em, Target here is pretty good." He patted the horse with affection. "In fact, I usually don't take the awards home anymore, enough is enough."

Emily was touched by the gesture. "Then I'd love to take it, thanks."

"You're welcome." He smiled, taking Emily's hand. "Come on, it only takes about five minutes for them to set up the next event."

They walked a short distance to a very nice looking motor home with a horse trailer hitched to it. There were several folding chairs next to the trailer.

"Have a seat. What can I get you? I have Coke and beer, and of course iced tea and even water."

"I'd love a Coke." Emily smiled at him.

"Diet or regular?" David asked.

"Regular, please," Emily replied ruefully, "I hate the diet stuff."

"Me, too." David grinned.

David walked into the motor home and brought out the Cokes. It seemed like the minute he handed the cold can to Emily, the announcer called for the next event to begin.

"Ain't that the way?" David stood up. "Let's go."

Chapter Three

They walked back over to the arena. The next event started without any surprises, but about halfway through the twelve and under age group a horse stepped on Emily's foot. David was right there as Emily gasped with the pain of having a thousand pound animal in steel shoes land on her.

"Just elbow him in the ribs and tell him to move his big as . . . ah body," he advised.

Before she could do it, David leaned down and picked up the horse's hoof, holding it high in the air as Emily moved her foot out of the way.

"Are you okay?" David asked.

"It's tender but I think it's all right," she told him, shaking and flexing her ankle.

"It's a good thing you wore boots." David was relieved.

"I borrowed them from Laura," Emily admitted. "She insisted I wear boots here."

"Laura's a very smart woman," David muttered with a strange look on his face.

"The next event is called Flying Figure Eight," David said as they got back to the job of opening the gate. "It's a run down to the end of the arena, with a figure eight loop around those three poles and a run back. It's fairly easy and the times should be quite fast, around 10 seconds each. The whole event should go fairly quickly. Then we'll run quadrangle. After that we'll have a lunch break." David smiled almost shyly then asked, "Will you have lunch with me?"

"Are you sure?" Emily said with surprise. "That's going above and beyond helping out the novice."

"I'd really enjoy it," David said gently, realizing that Emily was shy.

During the event there was an incident when one of the horses, another one of what turned out to be a relatively low percentage of arena-shy horses, backed hard into a sleeping horse tied to a rail by the arena entrance. The second horse, surprised and resentful at being awakened out of a nap, bit the first horse and pulled back from the rail he was tied to, fighting the rope. The rope broke and the already upset horse fell over backwards.

In spite of her fear of horses, Emily was scared sick that the beautiful animal might be hurt. She hurried over to the animal who was just rising to his feet, getting there even before David. Gingerly, she reached out and caught the end of the lead rope, talking quietly to the nervous horse. She looked down and saw blood running down the horse's foreleg just as David got to her.

"David, he's hurt!" Emily said in a shaky voice, pointing at the trail of blood.

"Let me look at him," David said, looking Emily in the eye. "Are you okay holding him?"

"Sure." Still, she surrendered the end of the rope gratefully when another rider came over and offered to help.

"He's okay." David straightened up. "It's a fairly minor cut."

Addressing the gathered riders, he asked, "Where's Mike?"

A young man jogged over. "I'm here. What happened? Someone said Max was hurt."

"He got spooked and broke his rope when one of the horses backed into him. I thought I told you not to leave him unattended so close to the arena," David said with a trace of anger. "His leg is cut but it's not too bad. If I were you, I'd bandage it up and take him home. Your saddle is pretty scraped up too."

"You'd like me to take him home, wouldn't you? Especially since I'm your closest competitor for the annual high point trophy," the younger man snapped angrily.

One of the other riders spoke up, "Don't be a jerk, Mike.

Your horse is hurt and it's your own darn fault. Do what's right for your horse and worry about the trophy later."

"You're right, Cap." Mike turned to David looking abashed and said, "Sorry about that. I was just upset. I really am more concerned about Max than any trophy."

"I have some bandages and ointment in my trailer if you need it," David said with no trace of resentment.

"No thanks, I've got some." He reached out and took Max's rope, scratching the big horse's head affectionately. "I guess you get the afternoon off, buddy. You probably did it on purpose, you lazy jughead."

"For someone who's afraid of horses that was really brave, the way you got hold of old Max and held him for me," David told Emily.

"It was nothing. I was just so worried that he might be hurt, I forgot about being afraid of horses," she admitted.

At that moment David decided there was something very real about Emily, something that made him want to protect and comfort her. He grinned to himself; she sure wasn't his usual type, but then maybe it was time for a change. Maybe it was time to look past a woman's appearance and into her character. In spite of her shy demeanor and underlying sadness there was an air of humor and kindness about her, and a gentle side to her nature.

After five or six more riders had gone, the very pretty blond woman rode up to David and handed him the reins to a large black horse she was leading around. She was covered with dust, her face devoid of make-up, and under her hat her hair was hanging in a long straight ponytail. She had on a western shirt, jeans and a pair of sunglasses that hid her eyes. Emily felt like there was something familiar about her but she couldn't place it. She also couldn't help feeling a little resentful that this woman could look so good even under dusty, dirty conditions when she herself didn't look that good on any given day in her life. Some girls have all the luck, she thought ruefully.

"Dave, you'd better get going, I'm after the next rider and you're after me," the blond said, then she turned to Emily and smiled. "I'm sorry, was I interrupting?"

"Emily meet Nicole, Nicole this is Emily." He made the introductions.

"Hi," Emily said softly, slightly intimidated by Nicole's looks.

"Hi Emily, nice meeting you." Nicole looked Emily over and then looked from Emily to David, openly curious.

David turned to Emily and asked, "Are you all right now?"

"Sure, I'm fine. Good luck." Regretfully she watched David swing up onto the massive black horse and ride away.

The rider in the arena came out and Nicole rode in. Her horse was like David's, very calm and well-trained. Nicole had a good ride. David was next and his horse was also well mannered. In fact, watching David ride his horse in, it was still hard to believe the horse could or would run at all. It was even hard to believe the massive animal was awake. David sat there, relaxed, barely holding the reins loosely in one hand, waiting for the arena judge to signal him that he could begin his ride. Just like the last event, when he received the signal, he took up the reins with both hands. As soon as he gathered the reins his horse visibly tensed, his powerful muscles bunched up, bursting with pent up energy. At David's signal he exploded through the course, running down to the end and winding a figure eight around the poles before running back to the timing poles and coming to a stop at the gate. David waited for Emily to open the gate and rode out, exiting quietly with his reins loosely held and his seat on the horse relaxed. Target was prancing a bit but he was very well-behaved. David gave his reins to Nicole who walked her horse and Target around, and he stayed near Emily while the next few riders rode and then went into the arena as the awards were announced.

They set up for quadrangle. The poles were set in a large square, with the timing poles in the center.

That event was much more fun for Emily. She had David's

comments to help her understand the action taking place in the arena, and even better, she had David's attention. She soaked up his attention like a dried up plant soaks up water. She realized that she hadn't even talked to a man in a long, long time except for her father's doctor, and he was in his sixties.

David only left her when it was his turn to ride in the event. Disaster hit when he came to the first sharp turn. Target lost his footing in the arena's soft dirt. The horse fell and of course, David went down too. Emily was shocked! The horse got up quickly but David laid there for a moment, dazed not only by the fall but because his horse had brushed his head with one of his sharp hooves as he scrambled to his feet. Emily left the gate to run to David, but she was only part way there when Target got up and trotted over to her. She grabbed Target's reins out of instinct and continued running over to David.

He was standing up, laughing ruefully, and he looked fine. He met her eyes and a spark seemed to flow between them. She ignored Target as she gently reached out a hand to the cut on David's forehead.

"Are you all right?" she asked with genuine concern in her voice.

"I'm fine." David smiled into Emily's eyes.

"You really had me worried." She looked up at him.

David looked down at the worry in her eyes and felt a slight tightening in his gut.

"I'm okay." He slid his arms around her waist in a quick hug.

Emily reveled in the brief, warm strength of his arms, hardly aware of the soft rubbing on her shoulder.

"Emily," David said with a laugh in his voice, "you caught Target!"

"Actually, he caught me. He just came over to me." She stroked the horse's nose unconsciously and said, "So I brought him back to you."

"Still, I think you're not nearly as afraid of horses as you think you are." He seemed to be fighting a laugh.

"What?" Emily gradually realized that both of David's hands were on her waist. The rubbing on her shoulder was Target.

"What's he doing?" she asked, with her eyes going wide.

"Using you as a scratching post," David told her.

"Why is he doing that?"

"Two reasons: He likes you," Emily smiled softly at that news, "and he has an itch he wants scratched. Just slap his nose and say NO if he's bothering you."

"I kind of like it." She turned and scratched the velvet nose gently but firmly.

David made no move to take the horse's reins from her, instead he gently said, "Hold him still for a moment, would you Emily?"

He bent down and ran his hands over each of the horse's legs in turn, feeling for any sign of injury or tenderness.

Then he straightened and looked at Emily. "Emily, do me a favor. Walk him straight away from me, about thirty feet or so. Then bring him back. I want to watch him walk to see if he's limping. I want to make sure he's okay."

She led the big horse away, with David watching for any sign of lameness.

When she led the horse back, David said, "Now jog with him the same way."

She took off at a trot, surprised to realize that Target was jogging right beside her. She turned and came back.

"Is he all right?" she asked with concern in her voice. "Is he limping? And how are you?"

"No, it looks like he's fine. He just slipped." David grinned then continued, "And I'm fine, now that you ask, but I might have a bruise in a real interesting spot and I'll probably be a little stiff in the morning."

"Are you sure?" she asked.

"I'm okay, Emily, the dirt's soft and Target managed to avoid stepping on me," David replied softly. "Although the big lug managed to scrape my head with one of his hooves as he got up."

They both walked towards the arena gate. David took the horse when they got outside the arena and left Emily to her duties while he walked Target around for a long time. This time, he skipped the awards ceremony altogether and walked over to Emily.

"Come on, you can join me for lunch. They have a thirty minute lunch break that usually lasts about an hour or so, and I have lots of food in the motor home."

"How can a thirty minute break last an hour?" Emily quizzed.

"I don't know, it's just one of those things, like missing one sock out of every load in the dryer," he told her.

"Or the fact that the pen closest to the phone is always out of ink?" Emily asked.

"You got it." David grinned. "Come on, let's eat. Believe me you don't want to eat the food they fix at the cook stand. I think the losing competitors wind up in the burgers."

"You're kidding!" Emily shrieked, laughing.

"You'd better believe it." David laughed at her expression, earning himself a playful punch on the arm. "These folks love their horses."

They walked over to where David had parked his small RV with the horse trailer. David pulled the bridle off Target and hung it on the saddle horn, then he hooked the left stirrup on the horn and loosened the cinch. He slipped a halter on Target. There was a big net filled with hay for him to munch on.

"Don't you tie him up?" Emily asked.

"Nope. As long as he has some hay, he'll stay put." David grinned. "I wouldn't recommend this with most of these horses, though."

"How is he?" She asked with concern. "Did the fall injure him?"

"He's walking fine." David knelt and felt the horse's legs,

finding no heat, swelling or tenderness in them. "And I can't find anything wrong with his legs. I'll see how he is after lunch. Let's eat."

David offered Target some water from a bucket and fed him a handful of grain and a carrot. Then he gave the big horse a pat and held open the RV door for Emily.

"Why did you leave the stirrup up?" Emily asked as she followed him into the motor home.

"So I remember to tighten the cinch up again before I remount. It's one of my old habits." He dug into the refrigerator. "You can wash up in there, through the bedroom." David pointed. "Would you like another beer or some iced tea with your lunch?"

"I'll take a beer." Emily followed the direction David pointed.

The bathroom was large for an RV, and the counter was filled with cosmetics. There was a large, well-lit mirror above the counter with a swivel chair in front of it.

Emily caught a glimpse of herself in the mirror and sighed as she began to wash her face.

How could any man spend time talking to her, she wondered. Her self-doubt doubled as she looked around the motor home and saw a small framed picture sitting on the dresser. It was a picture of a woman, a woman with uncommon beauty. She realized it was Nicole without the dust and dirt. Still, she seemed strangely familiar. No way she could compete with that, she thought.

Emily jolted with surprise. When had she stopped thinking of this as a pleasant interlude and started thinking of ways to compete for David? She might as well enter the Olympics. She made a face at the mirror and thought: Hey! I can be the Jamaican bobsled team of love.

Was this the kind of woman he dated? Emily gasped as she finally recognized her. The woman in the picture was Nikki Silver, one of the top models in the country. She was on the cover of at least one magazine a month. Her good looks were pure and classic: perfect features, flawless skin, and dazzling almond-shaped eyes, brilliant blue eyes. Shoot! Emily thought to herself, I should have realized David would know a woman like that. Stunning, rich, and famous, it figured, three things she would never be. Emily knew she was a good person, not perfect but fairly smart, witty and caring. She also knew that her outer appearance hid her inner qualities. How could she ever hope to compete with Nikki Silver?

When she walked back to the small kitchen table, David had already washed up at the kitchen sink. He had pulled several containers of food out from the fridge and had set out paper plates and taken the lids off most of the containers by the time she emerged.

There was a beer sitting by her plate.

"This officially doubles my beer consumption for the entire last year." She grinned, holding up the bottle.

"We'll sign you up for A. A. next week." He grinned back then said, "Have some chicken."

"I'd love some," she said firmly, "but first I want to take a look at that cut on your forehead."

"It's no big deal. That big clumsy lump out there just forgot to watch out for me when he was getting up," David protested, but he sat still and let her look at the cut.

"You're right. It's minor." Emily grinned. "Now I can enjoy my lunch."

"But that's not my worst injury," David protested.

"Oh really? Where else did you get hurt?" Emily was concerned.

"Where I landed." David grinned. "On my . . ."

He stood up and reached for his belt buckle.

"Never mind, in that case you'll have to take care of the problem all by yourself." Emily laughed, grabbing a piece of chicken.

"Darn." He grinned back at her with a mischievous glint in his eye.

Chapter Four

Along with the fried chicken, there was homemade coleslaw and potato salad, and a crisp green salad, biscuits with honey and butter, and chocolate cake. There was also some carrot and celery sticks, and cottage cheese. They sat there talking companionably while they ate.

"This looks fantastic." She sipped her beer then asked, "Do you always eat this well at horse shows?"

"Not usually," David smiled back at her. "I just had my sister's RV this time. She travels a lot. She also cooked the lunch, by the way."

"Then shouldn't we save some for her?" Emily asked.

"Not much, she cooked it for me." He smiled. "She loves to cook but she has a really small appetite. Thank goodness."

"I'll echo that." Emily grinned at him.

"So what do you think of your first horse show?" David asked her.

"Well, it's hot, dirty, long and yet fast paced." She paused. "I like it except for these darn jeans. I thought they were supposed to be comfortable but these are stiff as a board."

"Wash them several times with lots of fabric softener." David paused for a long swallow of his cola. "Not all horse shows are like this. Apart from gymkhana events, there are equitation events where horses are judged for their manners and riders are judged for their seat and hands. Those events are run in both Western and English divisions. They can be almost boring to watch unless you know what to look for. Then there's also show jumping, dressage and so on. This is just the tip of the iceberg." He looked at her with mischief in his eyes. "I already told you about the differences between horse shows and most other sports."

"Well, yes, you sit on poor innocent animals while you compete," Emily teased, then continued, "and men and women compete against each other as equals."

"It's a bit different in the judged events. There are trainers involved, and the trainers get clients by having their students win. So, of course, in some cases there can be favoritism. Still, there's a feeling of fair play for the most part. Most of the judged events have all the riders in the arena at once." David smiled. "That makes it harder to cheer on your competition."

"Back to gymkhana, do you like competing against women?" she asked, a teasing note in her voice.

"I don't mind competing against women unless they beat me," David grinned, "and believe me, that happens more often than I care to admit."

"What do you do when you're not riding in horse shows?" Emily asked.

"I'm a lawyer, mainly corporate these days but I also do a bit of entertainment law." He shook his head ruefully. "I used to do criminal defense, but I got tired of defending so many people who really did the terrible things they were accused of doing. Many times I thought they should be in prison or worse, which made it hard to give them the kind of defense I was obligated to give them and still sleep at night. What do you do?"

"I don't work now, I have obligations at home. I was just finishing my B.A. in business, going part-time, when things got so, um, messed up," Emily told him, the sadness in her eyes deepening.

"What do you mean messed up?" David asked tenderly, sensing her sadness. "You mentioned something before."

"Well, I have to take care of my parents," she admitted. "They're both sick."

"Both? That's tough. Tell me about them." His sympathy was sudden and real.

"Well, it's how life goes." She took a gulp of her soda and then explained, "My dad is a great guy, gentle and caring, and very funny. He's got this fantastic smile and a great sense of humor. He also has cancer, terminal cancer. He hasn't got very long."

Her voice cracked, but she gathered herself and continued, "My mother recently had a stroke, probably partially due to the stress of my dad's illness. She recovered the use of her limbs and her speech, but her mind is just not the same. She slips in and out of reality."

"So you're the caregiver for both of them?" he asked gently. "How did you get away today? Wait, I remember, you said Laura was staying with your folks."

"Yes." Emily was still quiet, reminded of her parent's problems.

"She's an inveterate matchmaker. Did she mention anyone before you came? Tell you about any of the club regulars? Anything like that?" he asked quickly.

"Not really." She shook off her sadness and grinned impishly. "She just mentioned that I should look out for a hunk named David." She paused, watching his eyes widen in surprise.

"Oh! Do you think she meant you?" she asked ingenuously.

"I can't answer that." He grinned. "If I say no, you might agree with me and that would crush my fragile ego, and if I said yes, I'd sound really conceited."

"Or truthful," Emily said.

"Thanks," David said smiling. "So does that mean you'll have dinner with me tonight after the show?"

"I can't," Emily said sadly. "I have to stay with my folks."

"Laura would be glad to stay with them," he grinned at her, "just tell her that her matchmaking worked."

"You don't want me to tell Laura that," Emily said with a touch of humor. "She'll believe it and she'll be like a shark smelling blood in the water, ruthless and relentless."

"Who said she shouldn't believe it?" Dave grabbed another piece of chicken. "Do you think it's so hard to believe that I'm interested in you?"

"Why should you be? You're very nice David, but why would you want to go out with me?" Emily's eyes dropped. "I mean I saw the picture in the bedroom, the picture of the model. If she's the type you usually date, I'm not in your league. She's gorgeous, famous and rich. If that's the kind of girl you like, why would you want to go out with me?"

"I choose the women I date because of their personalities," David said tightly. "Looks are nice, but if the personality inside isn't right, I don't date the woman. I certainly would never date the woman in that picture."

"And I wouldn't date him either. It'd be too tacky." Emily was startled to see Nikki standing behind her, grinning. "Of course, if David wasn't my brother, I just might."

"You're his sister?" Emily found it hard to believe that the woman standing in front of her, dirty and without make-up, was that same glamorous woman she'd seen in all those magazines but it was undeniable. "But you're a famous model."

"He's still my older brother." Nicole went over to grab the rest of the carrot sticks out of the refrigerator. She also grabbed a piece of fried chicken. "I have to run. Go out with him, Emily, he's not so bad. Really. He's a fairly decent guy with basically good table manners, and some women say he's a good escort."

She winked at Emily then continued, "I've even heard some of them say he's good looking, but I can't see what they're talking about. All I can say is he's not too bad, for a brother."

"Gee thanks." David scowled at her.

"Anytime." She stuck her tongue out at him. "Seriously, Emily, he wouldn't ask you out if he didn't want to go with you."

She sat down, peeled the skin off the chicken breast, and began to eat.

They finished eating and David brought out a chocolate cake.

He cut a generous piece for himself and one for Emily, then he looked at Nick and raised his eyebrows. She nodded with a smile, holding two fingers out with barely half an inch between them. Her slice was correspondingly small.

"Wow! This is good!" Nick ate her tiny piece of cake very slowly, savoring it intensely.

"It sure is." David ate his piece with gusto, Emily ate her piece slowly, almost reluctantly.

"I wish I had your willpower, Nicole." She looked at the model.

"Please call me Nick or Nikki." She smiled, her famous, dazzling smile. "No one calls me Nicole."

They heard the announcer call out that the next event would start in fifteen minutes. David then excused himself for a moment to check on Target.

"David, check my horse too," Nick asked before answering Emily. "If you had as tight a contract as I do, you would," she told her. "Willpower has nothing to do with it, really. It's dollars and cents. And I hate it. I like modeling, for now, but I hate the phoniness of it, the feeling that all I am is a collection of body parts. And the feeling that my only value is in this face I show the world."

"I can see what you mean, but everyone is judged by their appearance, and most are found lacking," Emily said with a hint of sadness in her voice.

"I know people can be cruel, but David won't judge you by your appearance." Nick stood up and began gathering up the plates and putting the leftovers in the small refrigerator. Emily stood up and helped her. "Are you going to go out with him?"

"I don't know," Emily whispered.

"What can it hurt?" Nicole smiled softly. "He's a genuinely nice guy, and I can tell he likes you."

"Well, okay, I'll think about it." Emily smiled back at her.

As soon as Nicole left the RV, Emily's insecurities began to mount up again. David came back in and told her the events were ready to start.

"David, why would you want to go out with me?" Now that he had asked her out Emily's thin veneer of confidence had fled completely. "I know I look terrible, I'm dirty and my hair is filthy."

"So before we go eat, take a bath and put on something nice. I'm not going into a restaurant looking like this either." He was patient.

"David, it's not entirely that. I have a lot of responsibilities at home. I may not be able to go out." Emily used another excuse, but it was a real excuse, based on fact.

"Couldn't Laura stay with them tonight?" he asked.

"Maybe." She sighed. "I can ask."

"If she can't, I'll take care of finding someone to stay with them. It sounds to me like you need to go out. So take a shower, wash your hair, and put on something nice." David smiled. "So when and where can I pick you up?"

"I don't want you to take me out because you pity me. I know that I'm not very attractive." Emily paused before continuing. Her voice was low as she finally added the dreaded words, "Besides that, I'm fat."

"I didn't ask you out of pity, I really enjoyed being with you today." David looked at her long and hard, noticing the sadness and low self-esteem she wore like an overcoat. He paused, estimating her weight at well over two hundred pounds, before adding gently, "As for being fat, yes, I guess you are, now that you mention it. I hadn't really thought about it. Even so, I've had a good time talking with you today. I like you and I'd like to go out with you, so who cares? Come on, at least give me your phone number."

"I'll write it down and give it to you later," Emily said as she rushed from the trailer, confused at his words and also by her reaction to them.

She quickly left the RV, walking past David to go to the gate. Nick walked over to David and took her horse's reins from him. As was her habit she checked the cinch, even though he had tightened it for her, and mounted. He mounted Target and they both rode to the warm-up ring.

"What's wrong with Emily?" Nick asked.

"I asked her to dinner and I think it scared her," David replied. "I don't think she goes out a lot. She's worried about both of her parents, because of their health. Also, I don't think she has a lot of confidence or self-esteem. She thinks she's unattractive because of her weight."

"The funny thing is, I'll bet I could get her a lot of work as a full figure model. She's got a beautiful face, under the dust. Good bones." Nicole smiled. "She'd be fun to work with." Nicole was planning to get out of modeling and into business as a physical trainer. "Let me know if I can help."

"Thanks Nick." David hesitated before he asked, "What did you think of her?"

"I liked her," Nick admitted, "but she seemed sad."

"Her parents are both ill, her father's dying of cancer. She's the sole caregiver."

"She's not your usual type, but I think I like her for you." Nick paused. "I'll admit, to my shame, that I was surprised when I realized you were interested in her."

"Me too," David admitted, "but I am."

They both looked over at Emily as she stood by the gate letting the twelve and under riders in.

"I mean, all the models that I've brought home to meet you. Who knew?" She looked at Emily again, shrugged and sighed. "She has a quality though."

"It seems like I'm not as shallow as even I thought I was because I looked into her eyes and felt that snap. The one you read about in all your romance novels." David grinned as they rode towards the warm up pen. "I'm surprised I never felt it before but I did today."

"Whatever you do, David, be careful not to hurt her. She has a lot of vulnerability and not a lot of experience around someone like you," Nick reminded him.

"I'm always careful of a woman's feelings," David said with just a hint of anger in his tone.

"I know, love, but be extra careful of Emily. She's different," Nick said. "And be prepared, some people are going to wonder why a guy like you is out with a fat girl and some of them won't be shy about saying it out loud, whether Emily can hear it or not."

Emily was fine running the gate by herself, but David went over to talk to her again when they set up the barrel race. He not only helped her learn more about how to assist the riders but he also explained about the event. He went on to give her more insights, a few humorous, into some of the horses and riders.

"See that big horse tied up over there?" David pointed.

"The brown and white one?" Emily asked.

"He's a pinto," David told her. "Watch the rider getting on him."

Emily was amazed to see a small girl of about four get on the pinto. "That little girl is going to ride that big horse? Is that safe?"

"For most horses, a child like that would be much too young to handle him safely, but that old horse has been around a long time and he has an extraordinary personality, just watch." David grinned.

The girl's parents led her to the gate. The girl rode the horse in, waited for the judge's signal and kicked the old horse. The veteran horse ran through the event with very little direction from the rider. He wasn't going full speed but he still had a better time than most of the younger riders.

"Don't ever repeat this but I think that old boy would run just as well without the rider," David whispered. "He only does one event."

"Why don't they buy the kid a pony?" Emily asked.

"Some ponies can be cantankerous," David told her, "and if they aren't, they become some kid's beloved pet. Then when the kid grows up he has to replace his favorite pet with something larger and faster. Guess what happens to the pony then?"

"He gets sold to another kid?" Emily asked.

"If he's a very lucky pony, but more than likely, he winds up as dog food," David said grimly.

Finally the conversation left the horses and went back to how their lunch ended.

David caught up with Emily. "Emily, why did you run out like that?"

"Because I don't want to go out to dinner with you if you're asking me because of pity," Emily snapped. Then her voice dropped and she continued, "I know men don't find me very attractive. And let's face it you're gorgeous, you probably date a lot of beautiful women."

"Emily, you don't know me very well but I don't ask anybody out because I pity them. Let's face it, I have dated a lot of beautiful women. It's one of the benefits of being related to a model. She brings home friends from work. I've learned that beauty is only skin deep. Some of those women are nice enough, some of them are very nice, but some of them are bitchy, or greedy, or just plain dumb. It's more than looks." David was finally irritated. "So I am very capable of seeing you for more than your looks. Not that your looks are bad. Even Nicole said you have great bone structure. It's just too bad that you can't do the same for me. You don't seem to see more than my looks. If we're talking about judging someone by their appearance, you're the guilty party. Think it over. I have to get ready for the next event. If you want to go out with me then give me your address. I'll be here the rest of the day."

Emily watched him walk away, suddenly feeling alone and more than a little guilty. She wondered if David really meant what he said. Maybe she was the one guilty of judging someone because of his appearance. She worked at the show for the rest of the day without any trouble. After lunch she switched from beer to her usual iced tea so that by the time the show was over she would be able to drive home safely.

She never wrote down her address and phone number. In fact, she avoided speaking to David for the rest of the day.

Chapter Five

Emily finally dragged herself home around 6:30 that evening. She was exhausted but she walked through the house to see what was happening. She found her father taking a nap on the sofa and she was careful not to wake him. Laura was in the den. After taking a deep look into Emily's eyes, Laura scouted out her husband. She found Jack in the kitchen with Emily's mom. They were cooking together and Laura grinned as she made a mental note to call for a pizza. She knew her husband couldn't cook worth a darn. She told him to watch both of Emily's parents before the two women went upstairs. Emily had to shower off all traces of horse before the smell made her dad's allergies act up.

"How was the horse show?" Laura asked, cautiously seeing the trace of familiar sadness in her friend's eyes. She also saw something else, something she couldn't quite identify.

"You lied to me, you rat," Emily told her with a wry grin. "I wouldn't get near the horses, huh? Well, I had to get right next to the horses. They put me on the gate in the gymkhana arena."

"Good grief! Didn't Kate tell them you were not a horse person?" Laura sat on Emily's bed.

"Kate and Bob weren't there, I think the kids were sick." Emily dug into her closet for something to put on after her shower.

Laura quickly called her friend. She talked to Kate for a moment and hung up her cell phone. "Her twins had the flu. She said she asked her friend Frank and Lanie to look out for you."

"I never saw Frank or Lanie." Emily sat by Laura.

"Probably because their daughter rides Western Equitation and you were up in the Gymkhana arena." She turned to Emily and asked, "So how did you handle working so close to the horses?" She seemed a little disappointed with Emily. "And why didn't you put up a fight?"

"The lady who sent me out there was more frightening than the horses," Emily admitted. "I was really scared at first, but finally I got some help when a horse pinned me against the fence and one of the riders came over and helped me. He explained the events, told me stories about various riders, and fed me lunch. He was very considerate."

She hesitated, looked, at Laura then continued, "He even asked me out to dinner tonight."

"A rider?" Laura was interested. "Who was it?"

"His name was David," Emily told her.

"David? A gorgeous hunk with wavy black hair and brilliant blue eyes? Rides a huge black horse named Target?" Laura was amazed because this was the best news she'd heard in a long time.

"That's him," Emily admitted.

"David Silvan asked you out to dinner? That's fantastic!" Laura absent mindedly rubbed her bulging belly. "He's one of the nicest guys I know, successful, and . . . Wow! He's such a hunk!"

"Aw come on, Laura. You know he's just being nice. How could a handsome guy like that really be interested in me?" Emily protested. "I mean, look at me."

"Cut it out! Sometimes I get so sick and tired of the way you put yourself down I could just . . . Look, David is really a nice guy, but he's not known for dating women out of pity. He must be interested in you." Laura grinned. "Just go take your shower, fix yourself up, and go. At the worst, you'll have a good dinner and maybe even some fun."

"I have responsibilities here," Emily said softly. "I can't expect you to stay any longer."

"Oh yes, you can." Laura laughed. "To give you a chance to go out with David I'd gladly stay for a week."

"And would Jack agree with that?" Emily laughed as she

realized that Laura's husband Jack would walk through fire if Laura suggested it. "Okay, don't even bother to answer that. Hey! I just realized I haven't seen my mom yet. Do you know where she is? Mom?"

"She's cooking in the kitchen with Jack, don't worry," Laura said as she noted the alarm in Emily's eyes. "I'll wind up ordering a pizza since neither one of them can cook worth beans. Your mom's flirting with him. It's kind of cute, she thinks she's twenty-five and she's after my man. Jack's having fun with her. He loves it. He's such a sucker for female attention."

"It gets old to live with, though," Emily confessed. "Sometimes she calls me 'Mom' and sometimes she calls me 'Sis'. If I'm lucky, she remembers that I'm Emily."

"That just means you really need to go out. Go get yourself ready and I'll take care of things here. Jack and I can stay until you get home," she offered.

"I didn't give David my address or phone number," Emily admitted, "and I think I made him mad."

"I'll call him. Trust me. Go take a shower." Laura grinned. "I'll be back in a minute to help you find something nice to wear. That dress you pulled out will never do."

"It's okay and I can dress myself." Emily was indignant.

"Yeah, sure you can," Laura said in a tone that clearly dismissed Emily's assertion. "I'll be here. Luckily you match my coloring well enough so my make-up will look good on you." Laura was in her element now because she loved matchmaking and pushing along other people's romances. She was also very successful at it.

"Go!"

Emily went into the bathroom muttering to herself: I can't believe she said 'trust me' again. Emily stood in the shower wondering if Laura would even reach David. He was probably mad at her anyway for leaving the show without telling him how to get in touch with her. No, she thought, he wouldn't be mad, he was probably relieved. She knew she just wasn't his type. It was a shame though, he really seemed so nice.

Emily took a long shower, shampooing her long, light brown hair. When she emerged from the shower she found Laura in her bedroom. Laura had rummaged through her closet and come up empty. She had put on one of Emily's skirts and taken off her print maternity jumper.

"This might just fit, if it does, it'll look better on you than anything in your closet. Here try it on." She held out the jumper.

"I need a blouse to wear under it." Emily moved towards her closet.

"No blouse, it'll look better. Put it on." Laura was stern.

Emily put it on. The jumper fit pretty well, except she couldn't fasten the top two buttons.

"Nice try, Laura. But it doesn't work. These buttons won't fasten and my bra shows. I don't even have a blouse to wear under it." Emily started to take the jumper off.

"For the last time, you don't need a blouse. Take off the bra, Emily. And leave the top buttons undone," Laura directed. "It looks better that way, sort of sexy."

Emily did as directed, then stepped back to look at herself in the mirror. The jumper fit snugly across her bosom showing her cleavage, then fell away in soft lines to become full and flowing around her calves. It was a floral print in shades of orange and yellow. Laura helped her with her hair, pinning it back with two little clips at the temples and letting it hang softly down her back. Laura used all her persuasion and managed to get a little make-up on Emily, just blusher, mascara, and lipstick, before they both went downstairs.

This time Emily's father was awake watching television. "Hi dear. How was your day? Did you have fun at the horse show?" He grinned. "You sure look pretty in that dress."

She went over to kiss his cheek. "Yes Dad, I had fun at the show. How are you?" She noticed the slight pallor in his face.

"I've been better," he admitted. "I'm having a little pain today."

Emily knew from experience that meant he was having a lot of pain. Although her dad seemed almost like his old self, he had lost almost fifty pounds in recent months. He slept almost all the time now, his hair was gone, and his color was awful. Emily and her father both knew that if he went into the hospital again, he would never come out. They both ignored it.

"I made a date but I'll stay home with you, tonight," Emily offered softly.

"No! You go out and have a good time," her dad said firmly. "Who's your date with?"

"A man I met at the horse show today," Emily told him, adding, "he's a friend of Laura's. Are you sure you'll be okay if I go?"

"I'll be fine. Now go on and enjoy yourself, you need it. Laura and Jack will stay here. I'll be all right." Her father paused. "I don't want you to shut yourself up in this house for your mother and me. That would just make me feel like more of a burden on you."

"Daddy! You two could never be a burden on me," she protested.

"Of course we are. I'm not stupid. It's a fact of life and it can't be helped." Her dad smiled sadly. "But tonight you can go out and have a great evening. You need some enjoyment now and then, it's very important to me. Okay?"

"Okay Dad." She kissed his cheek. "I love you."

"I love you too, Sweetheart." Her father smiled up at her. "And I want you to have the best of everything life has to offer. So go on, get out of here and have some fun."

Emily was filled with a mixture of conflicting emotions while she waited for David to arrive. She was nervous and still a little ashamed of herself for the way she had spoken to him. She was happy to be going out with him and yet she felt unworthy, as if he should be going out with someone who was better looking and more confident, more. . . More *something* than she was. She also felt vaguely guilty for leaving her parents again after being out all day. Even her house was a source of some concern for her. It was a comfortable house but it needed care: the lawn was a mess, the porch steps needed repair and the house itself needed paint. The interior was almost as bad: the carpet was clean but old and the furniture was getting worn, almost shabby.

Three years before, when they planned to replace some old furniture, her father's illness had been diagnosed. Ever since, Emily and her parents had saved money as much as possible in order to pay medical costs and just in case a private nurse was ever needed full time.

Soon David arrived, wearing a nice pair of tan slacks and a green and white striped polo shirt. Emily greeted him at the door. She took him into their living room and introduced him to her father.

"David, I'd like you to meet my father, Pete Ralston. Dad, this is David Silvan." Emily smiled. "David helped me at the horse show. He told me about the horses and events so it was more interesting. He even fed me lunch."

"I'm glad to meet you, Sir." David shook hands with her father; even to his untrained eyes the older man's illness was apparent.

"Likewise. Call me Pete. Can we offer you something to drink?" Emily's father looked David over and decided he liked this man.

"No thank you, Pete. Frankly, after spending the day at the horse show, I'm pretty hungry." David turned to Emily. "But I'd like to meet your mother too, if it's okay."

"I don't see how you can avoid it." Emily grinned. "Turn around David, she's standing right behind you."

David turned with a smile on his face and waited while Emily introduced him. "David, this is my mother, Mae Ralston, Mom this is . . ."

"I know who this is, I'm going out with him aren't I?" The woman in front of David was tiny, under five feet, with salt and pepper hair and pale blue sparkling eyes.

"No, Mom. David is my date," Emily said gently.

"Damn," her mother snapped. "Why do you always steal my man?"

"And why do you always think the best looking men are yours?" Emily muttered, not realizing that David heard until she saw his wide grin.

"If they're not, they should be," Mae said with a grin.

Laura watched from the window as Emily and David walked to his car. She dug out her cell phone. "Kate, you'll never guess what happened!"

She paused before saying, "Emily met someone at the horse how."

Another pause. "No, not Frank and Lanie. David Silvan."

She held the phone away from her ear as Kate shrieked. "No I'm not kidding, this is perfect!" She put her cell phone away.

As David held the car door open for Emily, she looked at him and softly said, "David, I'm sorry I avoided you at the end of the horse show."

"I wondered about that." David shut the door. "I was really disappointed."

"I was tired, dirty and I felt . . ." She hesitated, then took a deep breath and said, "Aw heck, the truth is I was overwhelmed, I couldn't believe someone like you could really want to go out with me."

"Someone like me?" he asked gently.

"Yeah, you must realize you're great looking and nice and well, just everything about you. I couldn't help but wonder what you could see in me," she admitted.

"You don't think much of me, do you?" he said with some heat.

"What do you mean?" She was surprised.

"If you think all I could see in you was your looks, you're implying that I'm really shallow," he told her.

"What more could you see?" she asked.

"I saw a woman with sadness in her eyes, valiantly trying to do a job she hadn't counted on even though she was very scared and uncomfortable. A woman who had the courage to be around animals she was afraid of, who ran and caught my horse without thinking of herself. She put others before herself, and did it without complaint and with a sense of humor." He smiled at her softly. "So put your insecurities away, okay?"

"Okay." She grinned.

"Then let's go have dinner." He started the car. "You look very nice, Emily, I like that dress on you."

She shot him a rueful smile and said, "Thanks." She paused for a minute before admitting, "It's really Laura's. It's a maternity dress."

"Emily, remember, don't be down on yourself. Whoever you got the dress from, you look nice in it. Really nice. Trust me." David seemed just a bit irritated.

Emily laughed. "All right already. I believe you. I'm looking good. How long have you known Laura?"

"What?" David thought a moment then said, "Oh, I forgot, the phrase 'trust me' is her motto."

"It's how she got me to the horse show," Emily admitted.

"It's how she gets anybody to do anything she wants." David laughed. "With her, that simple two word phrase is a lethal weapon and she's not afraid to use it whenever and wherever she wants."

"It's a good thing she only uses her power for good," Emily said. "I'd hate to think of what she'd do if she tried to rule the world."

"Instead she only wants to pair it up, two by two." David knew of Laura's matchmaking tendencies.

Emily was silent for a moment, thinking before she asked, "David, I have to ask. Laura's such an inveterate matchmaker, did she, um?"

Her voice trailed off with the question.

"Not to my knowledge." He grinned. "Maybe she has great intuition. After all she has a pretty good track record."

"No, she has a fantastic track record." Emily grinned back. "You may be in trouble, Sir."

"I'm not complaining."

Chapter Six

It was a fairly short drive to the outskirts of town where David pulled into the parking lot of a local steakhouse. The place had a casual decor and atmosphere, but excellent steaks and seafood. After they parked, they sat in the car for just a moment before getting out.

"Have you ever been here?" David asked casually.

"Yes, it's one of my favorite places," Emily told him happily, then her mood sobered, "but I haven't been here for years."

"Then I'm really glad I brought you here." He grinned.

When David reached for the handle of his door, Emily stopped him. "David wait. Before we go in I want to apologize again for the way I acted today."

David looked at her long and hard then said, "Which part are you apologizing for--thinking I'm a hunk," he grinned, "or thinking I'm too stupid to judge you by who you really are and not just your looks?"

"I never thought you were stupid!" she protested.

"So. You're apologizing for calling me a hunk or even thinking I'm a hunk. Somehow that's not too comforting," he teased.

"No! That's not what I mean," Emily protested again without thinking. "How can I apologize for thinking you're a hunk? If that was a crime all the women in Southern California would be in jail."

She noticed the slight flush on David's face before continuing, "I'm apologizing for letting my insecurities get in between us."

"In that case, apology accepted." David smiled and leaned

over to kiss her cheek.

He never knew how fast Emily's heart raced, even from that brief contact.

David got out and walked around the car.

He opened the door for Emily and waited as she got out. He closed the door behind her and took her arm.

They walked together into the restaurant. David had not called ahead because he wasn't sure Emily would go out with him, so they waited in the bar area until they got a table. While they waited, David offered Emily a cocktail.

"I'll just take a glass of wine." Emily smiled.

"Sounds great. What kind?" He looked at her, realizing, not for the first time, how expressive her eyes were.

"You decide," Emily told him. "I don't drink enough wine to know what's good or not. I do prefer white wine though."

"The house Chablis is pretty good here," he explained, "and I only want one glass since I'm driving. If you want more, please go ahead."

"One glass is all I usually have anyway," Emily told him. "I'll have water or a Coke with dinner."

They sipped their wine and talked until the hostess came over to tell them their table was ready. They followed her to the table and listened while she explained the specials. She gave them each a menu and left.

Soon a waiter came over and brought them water. He asked them if they wanted to order a drink, and they each ordered a Coke. He promised to be right back with their Cokes and to take their food order.

As soon as the waiter returned, carrying two Cokes, they each ordered a steak. She wanted hers rare and he wanted his medium well. The waiter left. Soon he came back with their salads, a basket of warm rolls, and a dish of real butter. Soon after their salads arrived a piece of conversation drifted over from one of the neighboring tables.

"I wonder what someone so gorgeous is doing with a fat pig like that? Maybe she's good in bed." It was a snide female voice, easily heard.

"Or rich." One of the other women at the table giggled.

David's face tightened and Emily reached out to cover his hand.

"Ignore them. They're ignorant fools," she said softly, but firmly. "And they're only questioning out loud what some of the others here are probably thinking."

"Now you know why I'm out with you," David said, his agitation making his voice get a little louder, "you're worth a hundred times more than a . . . a *witch* like that. Some people are really ugly on the inside."

He was rewarded with an audible gasp from the other table.

When he relaxed a bit, he looked at over at Emily mischievously and said, "I wonder if she was right."

"About what?" Emily was puzzled.

"The part about you being good in bed," David teased.

"How would I know? I've never. . ." Emily answered without thinking, then she shot him an accusing look. "That wasn't fair!"

"Well, if you ever want to find out . . ." he offered with a grin.

"I'll be sure keep it in mind," Emily shot back, her face red.

"Don't worry, I'll remind you." David's smile was wide now. "Fairly often."

The waiter brought over their meals and they both fell silent for a while, savoring the perfect steaks and stuffed baked potatoes. After a few moments they began to talk to each other.

Over dinner they had a long conversation. They spent the time really getting to know each other. The light conversation had one bad moment, turning more serious when they discussed why Emily didn't get out more often.

"You met my parents. They both need full time care and I can't afford a private nurse." Emily paused. "But I do get to go out sometimes, after all, look at today. I spent the whole day out of the house, and now I'm out again this evening."

"I know. And I can really understand how tied down you are," David paused before adding gently adding, "but you'll be a lot happier if you manage to take some time for yourself."

"I won't have to stay home forever. I'll have plenty of time for myself when . . ." Her voice trailed off weakly.

David reached across the table and gently covered her hand. "I know. It's not easy. And I'm not criticizing you, really. I'm just concerned. What happens if you wake up one day to find yourself all alone?"

"Then I go out and find a job, call up my friends, and find myself a life." She grinned ruefully. "Besides, I know Laura and Kate will gang up on me. They have a spotless record as matchmakers. Also, I have lots of plans. Things I'd like to do when the time comes that I can put myself first. I just pray it's not too soon."

Emily shook her head a little sadly then continued, "Do you think it makes me sound like a ghoul? That I've planned ahead, even dreamed of things I've waited to do, after my parents are gone?"

"Not at all. I think you need to have those plans and dreams, otherwise you'll find yourself adrift and that would make the loneliness worse." He added softly, "But I also think you can't live your life dreaming of the future. You need to find time for yourself right now. If you keep waiting for tomorrow to come, dreaming of how it could be, you'll be passing up too many todays. Life's too short as it is."

David paused, taking a sip of his Coke. "Can I ask, what are some of your plans?"

"I want to go back to school and finish my B. A., then find a job, join some social clubs to meet new people, maybe I'll even try to workout and get in better shape. Then I'll get my hair done, buy a new wardrobe and go on from there. Also, I've always wanted a dog, but my dad's allergic to them."

"Why don't you go back to school now?" David asked. "You don't have to spend that many hours in class, or you can take courses online and, of course, you can study at home."

"I can't afford a computer, and the online courses are still expensive. Plus, even studying online, I'd need to use the nurse once in a while and I can't afford the nurse that often. It's all too expensive." Emily had thought of taking classes and rejected the idea.

"Well, yes. The courses and computer add up, and I guess a private nurse would be pretty costly but daycare's not that expensive," David pointed out.

"Daycare? But that's for kids." Emily was surprised.

"No. There's daycare for seniors, too. The senior center on Main has a daycare from 8-4 on weekdays." David paused before continuing, "At least they used to. It was kind of neat. They do simple exercises, arts and crafts, sing, and play games. I don't know what it costs now, but when my dad was still alive it was very reasonable. It's worth looking into."

"You lost your father? I'm sorry." Emily admitted, "Sometimes I get so wrapped up in my own little world that I forget other people have problems, too."

"Dad was a lot older than most of my friends' fathers. Believe it or not, he was almost fifty when I was born, and close to sixty when Nicole was born. He passed away about three years ago." David grinned. "I have a lot of good memories of him. We were the last two of his six kids. Our mother was his second wife. She was twenty-two years younger than he was and she could hardly keep up with him."

"So how's your mother doing now?" Emily asked.

"She's dating a man about six years younger than she is." David looked around secretively then said, "Don't tell anyone I told you this, but I don't think her new man is half the man my dad was."

"Why do you say that?" Emily was curious.

"She lives in Florida with my older stepsister and my sister tells me that when Mom comes home from her dates, she seems restless, and at the same time almost relieved to be home."

"Sounds like most of my dates," Emily said ruefully. "The ones I can remember."

David reached across the table and gently stroked Emily's hand, giving her a wicked grin. "Well, I'll do my best to change that, but you have to help."

"How?" Emily was puzzled. "What can I do?"

"You can realize that I'm here with you because I want to be, and leave some of your insecurities behind. You can tell me what you'd like to do." He kept stroking her hand. "And you can keep smiling at me, just like you are right now. You have the most beautiful smile, it lights up your whole face."

He hesitated before adding, "In fact, if you could use some extra money, Nicole told me she could get you some work modeling."

"Me?" Emily was surprised. "Are you joking?"

"No, I'm serious. Apparently there are a lot of fashion shows and catalogues for larger women. It pays pretty well, too. And by the way, Nicole suggested it, not me." David paused. "Think it over. You've got to admit, she's got a lot of contacts."

The waiter came back and asked if they wanted anything else, adding "We have a terrific dessert menu."

"Let's have something," David said. "What would you like?"

"I usually love dessert but I'm pretty full." Emily smiled.

"We can split something," David suggested. "How about a hot fudge sundae?"

"Well. . . I hardly ever resist hot fudge, but no nuts," she told him.

The waiter nodded and left, only to return shortly with a huge hot fudge sundae, a second bowl and two spoons. Emily and David split the sundae and dove into it.

When the ice cream treat was just a memory, David said, "Now what would you like to do next? Is there anywhere else you'd like to go tonight?"

"I don't know what I'd like to do." She held up her hand. "Honestly. I'm enjoying just being here, talking." She hastily covered a yawn. "And, to tell the truth, I'm a little tired."

"Well, you had a long day standing in the blazing sun." David put his money on the table. "Why don't we call it a night, for tonight, and go out again on Saturday? Would you like to go riding with me?"

"Me? Riding? On a horse?" Emily was skeptical.

David laughed. "Or a motorcycle if you'd prefer."

He took her arm as they left the restaurant. "Or even both."

"I'd be too scared," Emily grinned, "to ride either one."

"You'd be safe, I guarantee it. Come on," he urged, "I'll even see if I can get Nicole to stay with your folks. We can have a picnic if you'd like."

"That sounds so bizarre, the world famous Nikki Silver sitting home and caring for my folks," Emily mused. "Are you sure she would?"

"Why not? She's not just a pretty face, you know, she's also a real person and my sister." He grinned. "Most of the time I even think she's pretty nice, so how about that picnic?"

"Only if you let me do the cooking, after all you're taking care of everything else. Deal?" Emily grinned holding out her hand.

"Deal." David ignored her hand and pulled her gently to him, enfolding her in a warm hug.

He drove her home and they sat in the car for a while, talking. At one point, David held Emily, comforting her when her emotions suddenly spilled over and she broke out in tears. It felt so good to Emily, being held and comforted, being able to let her emotions out, not having to be strong. Finally, her tears stopped. She and David talked for a while longer. At last, reluctantly, he walked her to the door.

"Would you care to come in?" Emily asked, hopefully.

"Yes, I'd like that." David smiled. "Besides that, maybe I can help keep Laura from giving you the third degree."

"Oh God. She will ask me a thousand questions about our date, won't she?" Emily bit her lip. "Do my eyes look okay? Will she be able to tell I've been crying?"

"No, you look fine. Laura will try to interrogate you about me but I don't think she'll see any sign of your tears. All you have to do is smile vaguely and ignore her." David leaned forward and kissed her gently, the merest fleeting touch of his warm lips against hers, but he felt a shock run through his body. "That'll drive her crazy."

Emily also looked slightly dazed as she opened the door. They went in to find Laura and Jack more than ready to leave. In fact, they were getting a little desperate. Laura was in labor.

She paused only long enough to ask Emily, "Did you have fun?" She looked long and hard at Emily and David before she whispered softly, "Aha . . ."

Then she gasped as another pain hit. "Jack, we're leaving, now."

The normally easygoing Jack turned pale and rushed Laura out the door.

Emily's mother came into the room and said, "I don't like to tell tales out of school, Emie, but I think that girl may be pregnant. I'm almost sure of it. Do you think they'll get married?"

"They've been married for quite a while, Mom," Emily told her gently. "I think you may have forgotten."

"Oh, yeah, I think I remember." Mae smiled softly. "When's the baby due?"

"It seems to be due right about now, Mom," Emily replied.

David helped her make sure her parents were settled for the night, then he said goodbye and left. As he walked out the door he turned and said to Emily, "I had a great time tonight. I hope you did, too?"

When Emily nodded wordlessly, he pulled her into his arms and kissed her. It was a soft gentle kiss, warm and friendly, not passionate but sweet. It also lasted a lot longer than the quick peck outside. Emily wished it would go on forever.

Chapter Seven

David and Nicole arrived on Emily's doorstep early Saturday morning. Her pulse raced as she let them in. She took them into the living room and introduced Nikki to her parents.

Nicole was a big hit with Emily's father, who recognized her from pictures in Emily's magazines. He was impressed and a little bit in awe that a famous model would 'babysit' for him and his wife, so that Emily could go out with David. Mae was a bit less welcoming, seeing Nicole as a rival for Pete's affections. Soon enough though, Mae settled down. Nicole offered to play cards with her folks, and soon Emily was forgotten as a game of Texas Hold 'Em got started.

Emily was wearing the same jeans she'd worn to the horse show, but they'd been run through the laundry several times and had lost that brand new stiffness. Along with the jeans, she wore a hot pink knit top, sleeveless, with a scooped neck.

"By the way, go upstairs and get your bathing suit. We'll soak in the hot tub after our ride." He looked into her soft brown eyes and teased, "Unless you'd like to go in without a suit?"

"I'll, ah, I'll get my suit." Emily turned for the stairs.

"Get a change of clothes too, so you can shower before coming home," David suggested. "That should prevent your dad's allergies from bothering him."

Emily wondered what David would say if he realized that she was more aroused than flustered at the thought of being in a hot tub with a naked David. She went and got her backpack out of the closet and quickly packed the bathing suit and a change of clothes.

She brought her backpack down to the living room and

handed it to David. Then she took Nikki into the kitchen and explained her parents' conditions and medications to her. She showed her where the phone number for the family doctor was, and Pete's oncologist. Of course, Nicole already had David's cell and home numbers.

They said goodbye to Nicole and her folks and went outside. As they stood by the motorcycle, David held out a helmet for her. Wordlessly she took it, and put it on. David put the backpack and the lunch Emily had packed into a compartment on the back of the cycle then he got on, holding out his hand to Emily.

Emily got on gingerly, sliding her leg over and fitting herself onto the seat behind David. Because of the trunk on the back of the seat, she really didn't need to hold onto David, but she did. She was grateful for the chance to slide her arms around his waist in a gesture that both of them knew was more of an embrace than any attempt to maintain her place on the Harley. Her hands roamed gently along his ribs, exploring his body through his T-shirt.

As she relaxed her hands lowered, coming to a rest on the zipper of his jeans. Suddenly she stiffened, quickly moving her hands up to a more respectable position alongside his waist.

"Sorry," she whispered, mortified.

"Sorry?" David was incredulous, turning his head slightly as Emily leaned forward to hear him say, "I was having the time of my life. You have my permission to put your hands on my, um, zipper any time you want to, on or off the bike."

He laughed as the cars whizzed past them then said, "But it's probably safer if you do it when we're not on the freeway."

"You . . . you man." Emily cuffed him playfully on the shoulder. "Just drive the bike."

They pulled off the road onto David's place. It was far enough outside town that he had room to keep several horses on his property. He stopped the bike at his house and they got off. Two dogs came out to greet then. A chubby Boston Terrier puppy and an Australian Shepard. David started to ask Emily if she was afraid of dogs, but held his tongue when he saw her reaction to them. She was laughing and petting them with such joy in her face that David was amazed. He had never seen Emily so happy.

"I should have warned you I had two pathologically friendly dogs at home, but I take it you like dogs," he commented.

"I love dogs," she grinned at him, "but you know my dad's allergic to them. I never get to be near them in case he gets a reaction when I get home."

"We've got that covered this time," David said, "so don't worry."

He led her into the house, dogs following. They put the picnic lunch Emily had packed in the refrigerator. Then they walked hand in hand down to the barn.

"David? Do I really have to ride?" Emily was getting nervous now as they approached the barn.

"Relax, Emily. I guarantee you'll have fun, and I won't force you into anything you don't want to do." He paused then said, "Ever."

"Oh, I trust you, David, sort of." She winked at him. "It's the horses I don't trust."

"How about if you climb up with me on Target for a few minutes and get a feel for the motion?" he suggested with a trace of a dare in his tone.

"Will that be okay?" Emily asked wide-eyed. "After all, you must admit neither one of us is exactly a lightweight."

"Target's a big, strong horse, and we won't ride him double for very long, just long enough for you to relax."

"Okay, it sounds good to me," Emily quipped bravely, "as long as it's okay with Target."

She followed him into the small barn and watched as he put a halter on Target. He led the massive horse out of the stall, looped the rope over a fence, and began to groom him with a rubber curry comb in one hand and a soft brush in the other.

"Can I help?" Emily asked.

"Sure, you follow me with the soft brush and smooth his coat down." He handed her the brush, explaining, "This is not just a beauty treatment, you know, when we groom a horse we also watch out for injuries like small cuts, swelling in his legs, insect bites, or just any tenderness."

"So it's a health treatment, too." She realized.

"It sure is." He showed her how to comb out the horse's mane. "Although, this part is more cosmetic."

He showed her how he picked out the horse's hooves, again pointing out how he watched for any small stones or anything else that could cause the horse to go lame. Finally he saddled the horse and led him out of the barn and into the arena. He threw the end of the lead rope over the horse's neck and told her where to stand so that he could give her a leg up.

"This time you ride in front and I'll get up behind you. I'll reach around you to hold the rope, unless you decide to do it," he told her.

Emily stood there nervously, but she was game. After telling her to bend her left leg back so that he could put his hands under her knee, he gave her a leg up. Then he grabbed the end of the rope and a handful of mane and easily swung up behind her onto Target's massive hindquarters.

"You okay?" he asked her.

"Fine," Emily said with a shaky voice, enjoying the feel of David's strong legs on each side of her, and of his warm, hard body up against her buttocks. "So far so good."

David put Target into a slow steady walk around the arena. He turned the horse several times with just the rope to guide the animal.

"How does it feel?" David asked with amusement in his voice as his hands rose quite a bit higher than her waist, almost up to her full breasts. "Do you like it better in front or in back?"

"It feels great!" Emily was surprised. "This isn't so scary after all!"

She paused, savoring the feel of David's hard body so close behind her, and the slow steady rock of Target's walk. "I think I'll have to try both positions several times before I can say which is better." She giggled, just a little. "On the horse, I mean. I'm not sure I'll ever want to drive the motorcycle."

Was she imagining it or was David getting awfully friendly with his hands? It was probably her imagination but she enjoyed the feeling of his hands so near her breasts.

"I'm going to speed him up just a little to what we call a jog. It's a very slow trot." He stopped teasing her with his hands and put the horse into a jog.

It was a very smooth gait for a well trained horse like Target. "A fast trot is rougher."

He showed her for just a few steps.

"The next speed is a lope, which is basically a slow running gait." He put the big horse into a lope and Emily was surprised to learn that it was a very smooth and pleasant gait to ride.

He slowed the big horse back to a walk.

"Normally, when you ride, you'd use a bridle to signal the horse when you wanted to turn or stop, but we're in Target's home arena with no distractions, and I know this old boy so well that I feel safe with just a halter on him," David said out of the blue. "This old boy gets excited when you pull on the reins, he thinks it means something's up. It's like a call to action for him. With this halter he knows he can relax and be lazy. I decided to use it in case you decided to take over. Most new riders get nervous and pull on the horse's mouth, which upsets almost any horse, but it really gets Target riled up."

He handed the lead rope to her. "Go on, you're in charge."

She steered the horse around, following David's directions on how to turn the horse.

"This is great," she gushed.

"Okay, pull back and say 'Whoa.' Then ease up on the rope when he stops." David waited while she did as he instructed. "You did real well. Even as a beginner, you don't pull on him or fuss at him."

He slid off Target. "So take him around alone."

Emily was surprised but she did as he suggested. She rode the horse around for a few minutes practicing turns and stopping and starting under David's expert tutelage. Then she followed his instructions and eased the horse into a jog. The gait she got out of the horse was not as smooth as the gait David had achieved, until following David's instruction, she gently tugged the rope and sat back on the horse. Soon Target eased his way into the smooth as silk jog he'd been trained for.

"I hate to say it but you'd better stop now or you'll be so sore tomorrow you'll hardly be able to walk." David grinned. "People who don't think horseback riding is exercise except, of course, for the horse, would be amazed after they rode the first time. If someone without experience stays on too long, they get saddle sore. If you get saddle sore it can be the most miserable feeling in the world.

"Then thanks for not letting me stay on too long." Emily smiled at him. "Who needs to feel miserable?"

They brushed Target off quickly and put him in his stall. David showed her how to feed him a carrot without getting her fingers bitten off. They gave Nicole's horse a few carrots, too. A third horse also got some. Then, hand in hand, they walked up to the house. David showed her where she could change into her bathing suit.

"Bring me your clothes when you get your swimsuit on and I'll wash them so you won't have to worry abut your dad's allergies acting up," David told her.

"But I brought clean clothes, remember?" she asked.

'I know, but the clothes could still cause your dad problems, so why don't we keep them here and just use them for riding?" he suggested.

"Good idea." She smiled, but her pulse raced as she realized that he meant it.

This was not just a 'pity' or a 'one time only' date; he planned to keep on seeing her! She hurried in to put the bathing suit on.

When she emerged in her modest bathing suit, David was waiting for her. He put her clothes into the washing machine with enough of his to make a full load.

They went out onto the deck and he handed her a tall glass of iced tea. "We still have to wait a few minutes before the water heats up.

"Why don't we swim?" she suggested.

He had a pool, too.

"If you'd like. I just thought the hot tub would be more therapeutic for muscles that just got some unaccustomed exercise." David swallowed his tea. "Not that I mean you don't exercise, but riding uses different muscles."

"You'd be right to think I don't exercise," she confessed ruefully. "It just seems like I'd have to exercise until hell freezes over to do myself any good."

"I'm not saying you have anything to change or that there's anything wrong with you, but Nicole is studying to become a fitness instructor so that she can get out of modeling when she gets tired of it. She wants to open a special gym, just for people who are heavy enough to be embarrassed in a regular gym. The goals would be to get more active and fit, build strength and endurance, not necessarily to lose weight. Although, in many cases losing weight would be an added benefit, a bonus." He paused. "She'd be glad to give you some pointers if you'd like. She also has partners, some of the make-up artists and fashion coordinators she works with, who want to work with the gym members and do makeovers to help them be more confident and at ease with themselves whether they lose weight or not. She thinks some of them wait until they lose weight to fix themselves up and that is just lost time to Nicole. She'd love to practice on you."

"Can I think it over?" Emily jumped into the deep end, savoring the lukewarm water. She swam a few laps the length of the pool then rested at the side.

"Sure, it's entirely up to you." David swam over to one side of the pool, then reached out and took a sip of his tea. "At least until you mention it to Nicole. If you give her half a chance, she'll pressure you like crazy. She's looking for guinea pigs to work on."

David swam over to Emily who was floating lazily at the side of the pool. He kissed her gently. "I mean it. I'm not trying to change you.

Emily finally realized what was bothering her about David's kisses. They were thrilling but they were also tentative and almost too gentle. It was as if he was afraid of scaring her just because he knew she was a virgin. She thought for a moment and decided that she'd put an end to that nonsense as soon as possible. David was not only the nicest man she'd ever met but he was also the best looking. There was no way she was going to let him get away with that overly gentle act for too long. She got out of the pool.

"I'm going into the hot tub for a while before we eat," she stated.

David got out as well. "Me too, after I put the clothes into the dryer."

They soaked in the hot tub for about fifteen minutes before getting out.

"Shall we lie out in the sun for a while before we eat our picnic?" Emily asked casually.

"Sounds good to me." David toweled himself off and laid on a blanket spread out on the soft, plush lawn. "Come on, join me."

Emily joined him on the blanket and stretched out next to him, one hand gently stroking the dogs that came over to join them. They talked lazily, letting the hot sun wash over them. Soon

David planted several soft kisses all over Emily's face. He stopped suddenly, pulling back after giving her one long tender kiss on her mouth.

"David," Emily said softly, squinting into the bright afternoon sun, "it's okay, I'm not that innocent. I do kiss men, you know. I even enjoy kissing men, at least, I enjoy kissing you."

She smiled softly and said, "It's just that I don't . . . well, you know."

"You don't?" David fell back on the grass dramatically. "Ah, shucks, Ma'am. Ever?"

"Not so far." Emily blushed.

"Just so you know, I'll be working on changing that," he warned her in a tender growl. "When it's right."

Emily just grinned.

Chapter Eight

"Well for now, we'll stick to just kissing." David pulled her into his arms, then spoke with his mouth up against her lips, "But someday, maybe someday soon, I'm probably gonna try to change your mind."

"Is that a promise or a threat?" she asked with her voice full of exaggerated innocence.

"It's both." He groaned but explained, "I've been trying to be a better man, lately. I've gotten more active in my Church and for me that means trying to be a better Christian, so I know it's a sin, but you're really hard to resist."

Those were the last words either of them spoke for a very long time as he took her into his arms and his mouth closed over hers in a kiss that was still gentle but also full of promise, passion, and chemistry.

He used his tongue to gently tease her mouth open and was surprised to feel the intensity of the passion in her response. He was also surprised at the intensity of the response she aroused in him. After a long time, he wound up lying half on and half off Emily, kissing her and nibbling her neck. His hands were sliding gently over her body. He rested his thumbs against the sides of her breasts. Then with a quick move he rolled over, pulling her until she came to rest on his chest.

"Emily? Emily?" he murmured against her mouth.

She pulled back her head and replied, "What?

"I think we'd better stop this if you don't want to . . . Ah, I mean," he paused, his usual relaxed confidence failing him, "maybe we should eat lunch."

"At the very least, I'd better get off you." She grinned, joking as she quipped, "I wouldn't want you to feel squished."

"Squished?" David laughed. "I don't feel squished, I feel aroused."

Suddenly she was aware of his hardness pressing against her.

"I can tell." She kissed him. "Isn't it wonderful?"

She stood up and reached her hand down to him. "Let's have lunch."

Holding hands, they went into the house.

"Why don't you grab a quick shower?" David suggested. "I'll empty the clothes dryer while you are in there."

"Okay, thanks." Emily went upstairs.

When she came back down, she felt clean and refreshed. When David went up to shower she told him to hand her his bathing suit. She rinsed out both bathing suits and hung them up to dry. Then she went to the refrigerator and started removing the lunch she had fixed. Soon she heard David coming down the stairs.

"David," she asked, "where are the dogs?"

"I shut them in the den," he told her. "It's not going to be much help for your dad's allergies showering and washing your clothes and all that if we let dogs get all over you now that you're all cleaned up."

"Makes sense, now next question." She paused. "Why did you suggest a picnic lunch if we were going to be at your house?"

"Because, my dear, I like picnics." He came up behind her and slid his hands around her waist, nibbling her ear. "What are we having?"

"I made roast beef sandwiches on french rolls, along with potato salad, some cheese and pickles. I brought some au jus so we can either have our sandwiches cold or warm them up and make them into french dip." She grinned. "I also brought apple pie for dessert."

"I'm in heaven. I love french dips. Let's eat!"

Emily sliced the french rolls then picked up a plastic

container of roast beef and au jus. "Put this into the microwave."

David followed orders. Then he turned and watched as Emily arranged the food on the counter, opening the bowl of potato salad, opening the plastic bags full of sliced cheese and pickles.

"Is the roast beef hot yet?" she asked.

"Yes, Ma'am. Any more orders?" he asked with humor, realizing that he was finally clearly seeing something he had only gotten glimpses of before: the real Emily, relaxed and totally at ease.

"Of course, warm up these rolls, and don't leave them in too long or they'll get hard." She looked at him wondering what was behind that expression on his face. "Do you want to use paper plates or shall we get fancy and use your dishes?"

"Let's use real dishes." David smiled, a sneaky smile. "It's Nicole's night to do dishes."

"Then we'll use paper, you brat. Nicole's doing enough for us today," she said with gratitude in her voice. "My father recognized her, you know. He was shocked to have a celebrity stay with him."

"Celebrities are people too." David laughed. "Even bratty little sisters."

They dished up their food and carried there plates out onto the patio. They sat at a big redwood picnic table and ate, talking and munching contentedly. Emily went in to get the pie.

"Do you want it warmed up?" she asked from the doorway.

"Sure, and there's ice cream in the freezer," David called back.

"Perfect, a man after my own heart," she said, smiling.

"You finally got the message." His voice was full of meaning.

Emily grinned to herself, absurdly happy as she sliced the pie and put it on plates. She put one piece in the microwave while she got the ice cream out of the freezer, then she took that piece out and put the other piece in. She scooped ice cream onto the pie, pulled out the second piece and scooped ice cream on it too. As soon as she replaced the ice cream in the freezer, she carried the plates outside. They sat side by side as they ate dessert.

"Emily, would you go to Church with me in the morning?" David asked.

"Can we take my parents to the Methodist Church on Wilkins?" Emily answered his question with one of her own.

"Sure," David agreed. "I usually go to the Lutheran on Central Avenue, but we can go to your Church now and maybe go to mine once in a while."

Emily carried the dessert plates into the kitchen and cleaned up.

"How's Laura?" David came up behind her and said, "I heard it was false labor last Sunday."

"But it wasn't last night." Emily grinned. "She had a little boy just after ten o'clock."

"That's great! Do you think we can stop by the hospital and see her when I take you home?" David was enthusiastic.

"Sure, as long as I call home first and find out how Nicole's doing." She looked at her watch and said, "We'd better get going though. Doesn't she have a date of her own tonight?"

"Unfortunately she does or I could keep you here a lot longer." He grinned. "It wouldn't be such an important date if she weren't leaving Monday morning on a photo shoot. I don't think she's too serious about this guy."

"Why do I get the impression that you're glad it's not serious?" Emily asked.

"Because you're as intelligent and perceptive as you are beautiful?" David returned the question.

"Don't answer a question with a question. Is there something wrong with this guy?" she kept probing.

"I get the feeling he could be jealous, maybe even obsessive," David admitted. "And I think he cares more about Nikki because she's a model than because of who she really is. I hope I'm wrong."

"I'd bet on your instincts. Let's finish cleaning up this mess and I'll call Nicole."

They washed the serving utensils and put the leftovers into the refrigerator. Then Emily called her house and spoke to Nicole before they got back on the motorcycle and headed for the hospital to see Laura and her new son.

"How are things at home?" David asked.

"Fine. Nicole has everything under control," Emily was pleased to report.

They reached the hospital and pulled into the parking lot. After checking at the information desk they headed for the nursery first, then Laura's room. When they arrived at her room, they found out that Laura had other visitors: her husband Jack and her friends Kate and Bob Simmons. They began to mutter something about coming back when she had fewer visitors but Laura would have none of it. Kate, Bob and Jack were promptly banished to the coffee shop so that Emily and David could visit.

Just as she left the room, Kate looked at Emily and David then turned towards Laura and gave her a thumbs up sign, "Good job, how did you manage it?"

Laura, wide-eyed, just shrugged.

Emily looked at Laura and said, "So. You did set us up."

"Honestly? No. I hoped you'd meet somebody nice there, and David's the nicest guy around, but I really never guessed . . ." Laura grinned. "What the heck, if you were going to hand out an award for Matchmaker of the Year, I'd accept. Enough of this, have you seen Josh?" she mentioned the baby.

"We sure did," Emily said. "He's beautiful!"

"Congratulations, Laura. He looks wonderful." David leaned over to kiss her on the cheek. "We should have brought flowers."

"Don't worry about it, Jack's brought me plenty."

"We can't stay long, Laura. Nicole's at home with my folks," Emily explained.

"At least tell me what you two have been up to today," Laura pleaded.

"We went riding and swimming," Emily told her.

"Horses or the motorcycle?" Laura asked.

"Both. And we had a picnic," David added.

"Anything else?" Laura persisted. "Did things get, um . . . Interesting?" She watched as Emily blushed. "Never mind, I know."

"Well, we'd better go," Emily said, squirming just a bit.

"Bye, Laura," David added. "We'll have to find Jack and give him our congratulations, too."

"Thanks for coming." Laura sighed as they left the room.

They left, finding Jack outside the door. David and Jack exchanged a few male comments, as though Jack had done all the work in producing the baby. Emily hugged Jack, and then Jack gave both of them candy cigars. They told Jack they had to get going and then headed for Emily's house.

They arrived at Emily's to find her parents and Nicole watching television. Nicole left in her car to go get ready for her date and Emily and David sat at the kitchen table talking.

"David," Emily started, "can I ask you something?"

"Sure. What is it?" He looked at her.

"Well, I was thinking of asking Nicole to help me work out like you suggested, but so far I'm only interested in seeing if she can help me with the externals, hair, make-up and clothes." Emily paused. "I even want to find out if she's right about getting a few modeling jobs. Let's face it, we can use the money."

"Sounds good to me. What's your question?" He was curious.

"Would she really be interested in doing that or would she be after me to make major changes?" She then added, "And what would you think?"

"I think she'd love to help you. In fact, there is a reason why she'd be more than happy to do it but it's her story to tell." He grinned. "And, get this straight, I like you no matter what. Got it?"

"Got it." She nodded, grinning.

David stayed a little while longer before he left. He gave Emily a goodbye kiss that knocked her socks off, and another, and another. They made a date for Wednesday evening.

Wednesday proved to be a wet, rainy miserable day. Riding, whether it was done on horses or motorcycles, somehow didn't seem like a very hot idea. Emily was so convinced that David would call her up and cancel the date that she was reluctant to answer the phone when it rang.

As she had feared, it was David. "Hello Emily."

"Hi David," she greeted him. "I guess it's too wet to go riding this evening."

"Well, we could still ride but we'd feel like drowned rats when we got done. That's why I called you," David admitted.

"Do you want to cancel our date?" she asked softly, fearfully.

"Hell, no!" he said loudly. Then he dropped his voice and said, "I just thought we'd change our plans to dinner and a movie."

"That sounds perfect to me." She was relieved.

"Fine, I'll be over in about half an hour. Nicole's still out of town, but I have a friend who should be reliable enough too stay with your folks. Unless you think they'd care to come along?" he suggested.

"That's really a sweet offer but I think Dad should stay out of this weather . . . and David," she paused, "I want to be alone with you."

"I'll be right over, you sweet talker, you." He was pleased.

David arrived a half hour later with a woman of about sixty, whom he introduced to Emily as Julia. It turned out that she was his nearest neighbor. She was an R.N. and had worked until recently as a private care nurse. She seemed warm and capable, so Emily left with David without a qualm.

David took Emily to the nearest movie theater and they bought tickets for the latest action thriller. David stopped at the snack bar to buy popcorn and sodas, but Emily whispered in his ear.

"I brought some popcorn and a couple of cold sodas." Aloud she said, "Let's skip the snack bar, they overcharge for everything in these theaters."

They found two seats near the back of the theater. As soon as it was dark, Emily pulled out the popcorn and the soft drinks. They watched the movie and munched, stopping occasionally for some sloppy buttery kisses. All in all, they saw very little of the movie. They saw just enough to decide that they hadn't missed much.

"Want to sit through the movie and not watch it again?" David asked, nibbling her ear.

"Let's go some place where we can talk," Emily suggested.

"Good idea." David stood up and held out his hand to Emily. "I know a quiet restaurant near here. We can have a cocktail and talk for a while before we eat."

"I certainly want to wait for a while before dinner after that popcorn," Emily said.

"I'm glad you didn't make any more, it was just enough, and it tasted better than theater popcorn, too." He kissed her as he held the car door then said, "It still does."

"I have a better idea than just sitting and having a cocktail," Emily offered.

"What's that?" He was openly curious.

"Let's go into the arcade next door and play some video games, or better yet, find a table and shoot some pool," she suggested.

"Emily? Are you a pool shark?" David was surprised.

She didn't answer, instead she just smiled, a soft innocent smile. They drove to a nearby pool hall and rented a table. Watching as Emily expertly racked the balls, David knew he had found the true Emily, the one hiding beneath her shy and rather prim exterior. He had a hard time playing up to her ability. In fact, he lost most of the games, but he did manage to win a few. Then they left the pool hall and went to a nearby restaurant and got a table.

Over dinner the conversation took a serious turn. "I may not be able to see you as often for a while, David. My father's getting worse, I can tell," Emily explained sadly, her eyes misting.

"Then, I'll see you at your house," he told her gently. He reached out and took her hand, lacing his fingers with hers. "I'll be beside you wherever you are, whatever happens."

Emily nodded, her throat too choked up for words.

"I have an idea," David said as they got up to leave the restaurant. "If the weather's warm and your father's up to it, why not bring him and your mother over to my place this weekend to see the horses? It might be good for them to get out."

Emily thought a moment then said, "Mom loves horses, she used to ride as a girl."

"Could she still?" David asked. "On a gentle horse?"

"I'd better check with her doctor, both of their doctors, before I make too many plans." Emily was more worried about her dad.

"I'll give you a call on Friday to find out what they said," David told her.

True to his word, David called her on Friday. Emily told him what her mom's doctor had said.

"He reminded me that it was Mom's short-term memory that was affected. She probably remembers how to ride very well, that happened over twenty years ago. He also said that as long as she didn't take a hard fall, she'd be fine. Her only physical health problems involve her lungs, and even they aren't too bad yet." Emily paused. "Dad's doctor said it was okay for him to go too. He even gave me some antihistamine's that should ease his allergies." Her voice quivered as she added, "Actually, he more or less said it couldn't make his condition any worse so just try to keep him happy."

"I wish I was there right now beside you, you sound like you could use a hug and even a good cry," David told her. "Unfortunately, I had to take a business trip so I'm calling you from Toronto. I'll fly home if you want me to."

"Thank you, David," she replied, "but I'm okay. The offer's enough to make me feel better. When will you be home?"

"Unfortunately it looks like I'll have to stay over until at least Monday, which means we have to postpone our date until next weekend or even the week after." David paused. "I was looking forward to spending some time with you this weekend instead of being stuck in this hotel."

"Well, finish your work and come home as soon as possible. I miss you, too," she admitted softly.

Chapter Nine

The next day, Saturday, Emily had a surprise visitor. Nicole had returned from her modeling assignment and came over to see her. She greeted Emily's parents with affection and then she and Emily sat alone in the living room so they could talk.

"So what's new, Emily?" she greeted Emily.

"Nothing much. David and I went to a movie, and his next free weekend we're going to take my parents over to see the horses," Emily informed her.

"That should be fun," Nicole said. "It would be great for your parents to get out of the house."

"How about you?" Emily asked. "What's up?"

"Well, about a year ago I nagged and threatened my agent until I got some time off which, as it turns out, is right now. That's really why I'm here." Nick paused. "I wanted to get to know you since you seem to be important to David. I also wanted to talk to you about a project I'm working on."

Nicole seemed to be considering how to continue.

"The gym for people who are uncomfortable in regular gyms? The diet and exercise program?" Emily suggested.

"Well, yes. That and doing some full figure modeling," she admitted.

"Nicole, I'm still not sure that I'm ready to commit to a diet and exercise program but I'd like to give it a try," Emily said. "It's the only way I can find out how I feel about it."

"That's great, Emily," Nicole said. "We've got the gym set up and we're almost ready to open. You can be our test client. I want my gym to be welcoming to those who are overweight and who want to have a place where they can work out and be treated like they are special."

"That sounds wonderful. How hard is this program going to be?" Emily asked. "I'm not lazy but I have so many commitments. . ."

"We'll tailor a program just for you." Nicole smiled. "We'll stick to working out to improve your health and relieve your stress instead of doing a 'boot camp' designed to torture you into shape. I have an idea of how we can start that might drive David a bit crazy."

"What is it?" Emily was intrigued.

"We can start by doing things that are fun, not like real exercises. We can swim and I can teach you to ride, without telling David. Then we'll surprise him."

"That sounds good to me." Emily grinned. "Who can stay with my folks?"

"You met Julia, the RN, she would be glad to do it," Nikki said.

"Okay," Emily paused then asked, "and how about the diet? Do I have to give up all my comfort foods?"

"We'll look into what foods you like to eat and how we can manage your diet without making it impossible to stick to." Nicole grinned. "That's why we need a guinea pig, to work these things out."

"And I've decided one more thing," Emily said firmly.

"What's that?" Nicole shot her a questioning glance.

"Well, I've decided that if the offer is still open, I'd like to have you help me with a makeover. Teach me how to pick the right clothes, do my hair and make-up." She stood up and walked around the room.

"Great! Let's do a makeover and shoot a few pictures so that I can talk to my agent about you," Nicole suggested.

"David said you wanted to see if I could model but I thought he was nuts." Emily was still surprised at the outlandish idea.

"He is nuts, but in this case he's right." Nicole paused. "Like I said, most of what the fashion industry calls full figured is still what most women call skinny, but there are a few places where a larger model does quite well. As for the rest, I'm smart enough not to try to talk you into anything you're not ready for, but let's give it a try and have some fun, okay?"

"Okay, I guess." Emily turned to face Nikki.

"Such enthusiasm." Nicole laughed. "Can I use your phone?"

In a surprisingly short time, Julia was caring for her parents and Emily found herself out at the ranch. She was shocked when Nicole brought out the horse she didn't know and tied him to the rail.

"Who is this?" Emily asked. "I thought I'd be riding your horse or Target."

"This is Midnight Raider. He's green, which means he's not really well trained, but he's very gentle and safe. You can learn things together." Then she went in to get her own horse.

Nicole turned out to be wonderful instructor. She was patient and cheerful. She showed Emily everything from mounting correctly to dismounting. She had Emily work the horse at a walk and soft jog. After a few days she had Emily cantering. Before long, she had showed Emily how to lope figure eights, with a lead change in the center. Then she suggested that Emily try trotting through the poles and barrels set up in the arena.

"Concentrate on riding through the course smoothly instead of thinking about speed," she told Emily.

After each ride they took a swim, doing laps instead of just floating around. After about a week Emily found herself loping through the gymkhana courses. It felt thrilling to Emily even without real speed.

"I can't wait to show David, he's going to be shocked," she gushed, floating in the pool.

"Just remember, it's a surprise until he can see it. I know you talk to him every night." Nick stopped swimming then softly said, "And I know he prays with you, for your folks. I pray for them every night, too."

"On one hand, I can't believe I found someone to share this with, it's been so hard alone," Emily said with a soft sigh. "On the other hand, it feels so natural, as if it's meant to be."

"I'm sure it is meant to be," Nick said as she started swimming again.

"Whatever happens with David, I'll always thank God for both of you." Emily stopped floating and began to swim.

"Emily, since we're already into swimming and riding, how about starting the day in the gym downtown?" Nicole suggested. "Then we can come out here and ride to relax."

"Sure, I'll give it a try," Emily agreed, "but I have to watch the time."

"I know. Tomorrow I want to do the makeover and photo shoot, so we'll skip a day at the ranch. Okay?" Nicole smiled. "The photographer I have lined up has to leave town the day after tomorrow, so tomorrow's the day."

"Tomorrow then, I hope I don't lose my nerve." Emily hit the edge of the pool and turned.

The next day Nicole picked Emily up and took her to the gym. The gym was almost ready to open. It was a surprisingly cheerful atmosphere with bright colors and soft lighting. There were pictures on the walls and soft rock music in the air.

First, Emily changed into her workout clothes and Nicole took her picture, measurements and weight, all without letting Emily see the results. Then Emily followed Nicole around, testing each machine, and learning about things like reps and intervals. She learned how to check the weights on each apparatus and how to adjust them so they were right for her.

Then, after a short workout, she showered and dressed. Nicole took Emily next door to a photography studio that her friends owned. Almost as soon as they entered the studio Nicole and a photographer named Hans were discussing Emily's face, coloring and hair with a hairstylist and a make-up artist.

"Emily," Nicole said, noticing a trace of panic on Emily's face, "we're ignoring you, I'm sorry. In this business we get into the bad habit of discussing the person we're working on almost as though they weren't there. In modeling it's as if the model is a set of body parts, not a person. I guess if we're going to work with private citizens as clients we're going to have to be more sensitive."

"That's okay," Emily told her, "I guess that's why you needed me as a guinea pig."

"We're going to do three sets of shots. First, we'll do some everyday looks with just a touch of make-up and a real easy, low-maintenance hairstyle. We'll shoot you in casual clothes. Then we'll show you how to dress up your hair and make-up for a business environment, how to dress for success. We'll shoot you in some business suits and dresses. Finally, we'll do some high fashion shots with complete high fashion hair and make-up, and shoot you in an evening gown."

Almost before Emily knew what was happening to her, she was sitting in a beautician's chair getting her hair cut and styled. Then it was sectioned and highlights were put on. Her hair was being brushed and blow dried as the make-up artist gave her a manicure. Finally, the make-up artist applied a light dusting of blush, some eyeliner and mascara, and a deep rose colored lipstick to Emily and she was given a wide print skirt and a bright knit top to wear, along with a pair a strappy sandals.

The final result looked cool and comfortable, yet crisp and sharp. Emily's hair fell in soft waves, slightly below her shoulders and she had soft bangs across her forehead.

"You look great, Emily," Nicole told her enthusiastically. "Do you like it?"

"It looks great!" Emily worried, "But will I be able to keep it up?"

"Sure, this is all easy maintenance. I'll show you how to do it," Nikki volunteered.

The photographer shot a few shots of Emily on artificial grass in a picnic setting. It reminded Emily of the lunch she had made for David and she found herself daydreaming about that day.

"She's a natural in front of the camera. I thought we'd have to coax her into relaxing but she's perfect." The photographer was practically gushing.

"She's great!" Nicole agreed. "I'm shocked, and I suggested it."

"I'd give half a million dollars to find out what was causing that expression on her face," the photographer whispered to Nicole.

"I hope that expression has something to do with my brother, David," Nicole whispered back.

The photographer finished his shots and told them to get ready for the business set-up. Emily found herself being worked on again, her face was cleansed and redone, this time with a warm beige liquid foundation and a light powder. Again it was topped off with mascara, eye shadow, blush, and lipstick. Her hair was pulled and twisted into a classy French roll. She was given a new set of clothes to wear. This time, a well made support bra, panties with tummy control and sheer hose over all that. She had a soft tan business suit with a soft peach silk blouse. She wore heels that matched the suit, a gold necklace, and small shell shaped earrings completed the outfit.

This time the photos were shot in an office setting. They shot Emily standing next to a file cabinet and then sitting at a desk working, even one with Emily sitting with her back to the desk, leaning back in her chair with the phone up to her ear, laughing. Again, Emily had no hesitation in front of the camera.

Finally, Emily was put through the mill again. Her face stripped of all make-up, her hair set in rollers. Everyone ate lunch except Emily, the hairdresser and the make-up artist. Finally, Emily was ready to dress. This time she was not even allowed to see her face when it was done but it seemed to Emily that the Sistine Chapel had probably been painted in less time. She was given a different bra to wear under her evening dress, it was a push-up bra that accentuated her cleavage. The dress was a vibrant, hot red. It had a fitted bodice, heavily beaded, and then fell away in soft folds. The neckline was daring, cut very low and square, revealing more cleavage than Emily ever had before. She had black high heels and black lace hosiery. To set it all off, she had a stunning necklace that she sincerely hoped was not made of real diamonds and rubies, and long hanging matching earrings. Last of all her hair was combed out into a fluffy mass of wavy curls.

"It's a shame we didn't get a guy in a tux to pose with her," the photographer muttered as he maneuvered Emily into position.

"If we had, David would kill us," Nicole told him.

"Like that, is it?" he answered back. "David's not usually the jealous type. I'll say this for him though, he can sure spot quality."

Hearing this, Emily added, "Especially because I was covered with dirt and grime when we met."

"Maybe we should have made her up in the grunge look." Hans laughed.

After a few shots, they put her in another dress. This one was tangerine. The make-up artist and hairstylist left. Emily was posed in a new setting.

Finally, with a little firm persuasion on Nicole's part, they shot a few shots of Emily in a black lace nightgown and peignoir set.

"You guys don't think you're going to get me to pose, um, topless do you?" Emily asked suspiciously when Nicole told her to remove the peignoir.

They both flushed slightly as Nicole rushed to explain to Emily, "I just thought you'd like a few boudoir shots, nothing topless, just a tad bit racy in case you wanted to give them to, umm, someone as a gift."

"Besides, if you want to model, you'll need some lingerie shots for your portfolio," Hans added.

"Oh, that's okay then." In a move that surprised both Nicole and the photographer, Emily removed the peignoir and let one slender strap of the nightgown slide off one of her shoulders and down onto her arm.

She posed standing there, then posed for several shots on the stage bed in the background. In several shots, the nightgown seemed to be poised at the very brink of falling completely to her waist. In one final shot she crossed her arms under her breasts, pushing them together and up, almost out the top of the gown. In the last shot she turned her back to the camera, then turned her head to wink at Nicole and the photographer as she let the gown fall to her waist. The photographer snapped the picture just as the gown seemed to be caught on her hips before falling gently to the ground.

With her back still to the camera, Emily bent over and pulled the gown back into place before it fell completely.

She turned to a stunned Nicole and said with a grin, "Good enough?"

"My God. Emily! Whoever told you that you were shy was an idiot. You're a natural!" Nicole was enthusiastic.

"I got some great shots, wait until you see them." The photographer was excited. "You two go away for a while so I can get these developed."

"Why don't you bring them to Emily's when they're ready?" Nicole suggested.

"Do you have any wine?" Hans asked Emily.

"Sure," Emily lied shamelessly.

"Any spaghetti?" Hans asked.

"I can fix some," she replied.

"I'll have the proofs there by eight. Just give me the address," Hans said with enthusiasm.

"I do know that for a session like this you could charge a lot more than wine and a spaghetti dinner," Emily said softly. "All those poses, with a whole team working on me. I really want to thank you."

"It was no problem, we had fun," Hans told her. "And remember, if we sell some shots we'll get a cut, so that's fair."

Emily changed back into her own clothes then got into Nicole's sports car. They planned to stop at a grocery store on the way home.

Chapter Ten

As they drove home, they talked some more and Emily had one request for Nicole.

"Nicole, please don't tell David about the photos just yet," she asked. "I want to surprise him, at least I want to if any of these came out okay."

Nicole laughed then said, "Em, I think you're going to be the one getting a surprise!"

They stopped at the store and bought some groceries. Emily was startled to realize how Nick had to hide herself just to avoid being noticed. She put on a stocking cap, tucking her hair up and out of sight, then she put on large sunglasses that covered her face. She walked into the store with her head down, avoiding eye contact with anyone.

"Do you have to do that all the time," Emily whispered to her, "hide yourself to avoid being noticed?"

"I don't do it around my home in the stores where I usually shop. They're used to me," Nick explained. "And when I have time, I just take the chance I'll be noticed and have a fan come up to me. I really don't mind as long as I'm not in a hurry. It's the price I pay for being a model. Most of the fans are nice. I run into a lot of young girls who want to be models, so I take time to talk to them. I explain the difficulties and the pressures of the job but still I've given a few of my agency's business cards out. This time I wanted to avoid the distraction so we can get home and cook."

"Do you ever get the other kind?" Emily asked quietly. "The fans that are just plain nuts or even scary?"

"It happens." Nicole went silent.

They bought a couple of bottles of wine, lettuce and other ingredients for a field salad, bottled salad dressing, garlic bread, and ingredients for Nikki's spaghetti sauce. Emily grabbed a cheesecake at the store's bakery.

Emily and Nicole, along with Emily's mother had a ball fixing the spaghetti. As they worked, Nicole questioned Emily about her relationship with her brother David. Although she hardly made any comments, Nicole read most of what she needed to find out in Emily's face.

"Nicole," Emily asked tentatively, "if I let you put me on a diet and exercise program, how severe would it be? Would I have to starve myself to death and work out like I was in training for the next Olympics?"

Nicole laughed. "Not really. I have an easy start program. One that's also easy to stick to because if it's not practical and fairly easy, you'll give it up."

"I'll email you a copy of the plan but basically here's what I'm suggesting. . ." She went on to tell Emily her basic plan. "First, analyze your eating habits and find one or two things you can eliminate from your diet forever. Give them up completely. Say for example, colas or potato chips. Whatever you know you can do without."

"Salads and veggies?" Emily was only partly teasing.

"No way, Jose." Nicole was firm. "Give up the good stuff. In fact, you need to add a couple of things to your diet, things like more fruits and veggies. Now for the next thing, write down everything you intend to eat *before* you eat it. Carry a notepad everywhere you go."

"Okay." Emily nodded.

"And make sure to have a cup of soup and salad with low fat dressing before you move on to your meal. Except at breakfast, of course. Then go to your vegetables at lunch and dinner, then your entree. Also, as silly as it sounds, remember to quit eating when you feel full. No stuffing yourself."

"So far, I can do it," Emily commented. "It doesn't sound too scary."

"Also, allow yourself a dessert once a week, but no more than that. When you want to treat yourself to something special, make sure it's not food. Try other things like new clothes or shoes, perfume or a CD, stuff like that." Nicole paused, then continued slowly, "And don't use food for comfort. I think that part may be hard for you."

"I do use food as a comfort or a treat," Emily admitted.

"Two more things: First, don't weigh or measure yourself too often. In fact, I'd use your measurements instead of your weight to track your progress. And lastly, work out." She paused as Emily groaned. "You're already doing most of it. You ride and swim almost daily now. Just add to that gradually. Take a walk or use a treadmill, and build up both your speed and distance. Also work on strength training to build firmer muscles. Muscles actually burn calories faster than fat. Of course, it's great that you've already found out how much you enjoy swimming and horseback riding. Just keep those two things up, and work out in the gym when you can. Try to enjoy yourself, and the workout. Work on getting yourself healthy, and try not to focus on losing weight."

"It sounds like a lot of work but also it sounds very sensible," Emily commented. "And I love the swimming and horseback riding. It's more fun than a workout, and my clothes are already getting looser."

"Gee, I wonder how that happened." Nick grinned.

"You're devious, you fiend." Emily laughed. "I like that about you."

"Of course, you should have a doctor check you out before beginning all of this, although this is basically just healthy advice," Nicole concluded.

"That's all?" Emily was amazed.

"Think it over. I'll bet it turns out to be enough. That is if a slow weight loss and a gentle firming of your muscles is enough."

Nicole paused. "The problem is, most people who want to diet, want to crash. They need instant gratification or they get bored and give up."

"That's the trap I always fall into, I get impatient," Emily admitted. "I'll give your plan a try. Let's set the table."

With the ease of old friends instead of new acquaintances, they set the table and laughed over Nicole's stories about life as a model. With the ease of old friends instead of new acquaintances, they set the table and laughed over Nicole's stories about life as a model. Then they sat at the kitchen table with a glass of wine waiting for Hans.

Emily finally asked Nicole a question that had been puzzling her. "Why do you want to get out of modeling and into running a fitness center?"

"Let's face it. I've been blessed with a face and a figure that sells products," Nicole sipped her wine, "but it's not like I cured cancer or solved global warming. I know of girls who go to extremes to get thin thinking that they can have it easy. They diet to the point of anorexia, some get hooked on pills, and there are even some who kill themselves if they can't get to that *perfect* look."

"My God." Emily was shocked. "That's so sad."

"It's pointless too." Nick continued, "That easy life is not so easy. I have to model swimsuits in January, coats in July, plus I have a very erratic schedule, either working long hours or wondering when the next job will come along."

"I can't believe you have to sit and wait very often." Emily laughed.

"Well, not yet but I'm getting older and in modeling being young is almost as important as being thin." Nicole finished her wine just as they heard a knock at the door. "That must be Hans."

Emily went to the door to let Hans in. Aside from the pasta they had everything ready. The salads were made, the spaghetti sauce was simmering, and the water for the pasta was waiting on the stove. Emily opened more wine and served Nikki and Hans, then turned on the stove.

After introducing Hans to her parents, they decided to eat dinner before getting out the photographs. They sipped the wine while the pasta bubbled. Then everyone was seated and Emily served dinner. Emily was so nervous about seeing the photos that she could hardly eat. Although she knew these would be excellent shots done by a top fashion photographer, with the help of professionals doing her hair and face, she knew what she looked like. I'm sure no raving beauty, she thought to herself, and no matter what they did to me, it's still going to be me. Don't let it matter so much, she thought. Still, she hoped she would see something to give her optimism for the future, a taste of confidence in herself.

As soon as they had finished eating dinner and cleared the dining room table, Hans brought out the pictures. The first group he brought out, the casual picnic shots, were great. Emily looked relaxed and natural in the pictures, not posed. Hans had made 8 x 10 prints of two of the poses, and he had a proof sheet with the rest of the shots.

"I thought these two were the best, but some of the others came out very good too." Hans showed her the prints and the proof sheet. "What do you think?"

"I never thought anyone could take pictures of me that looked this good." Emily smiled softly. "Thank you Hans."

She handed them to her father.

Pete looked at the pictures and passed them to Mae. "These are beautiful, darling, but I've always seen you that way."

"This is a real pretty girl," Mae said. "Why don't you bring her over sometime?"

"That's me, Mom," Emily said gently.

"By golly, it is." Mae smiled. "You look real good, Sis."

Emily looked at Nicole and Hans with a sad grin and said softly, "Close enough."

Hans brought out the business shots. Once again, he had printed two of the shots in 8 x 10s and he had the rest on proof sheets. In the first shot, Emily sat at a computer; she looked cool and professional. In the second, the shot with her chair turned away from her desk as she leaned back and laughed into the phone, her hair was beginning to come out of the bun. It was just a few tendrils, but the effect made her look like she was taking a break after a long hard working day, flirting with an unseen man over the phone.

"Is it possible for me to say thank you too many times?" She looked at Hans with her eyes shining.

"Hold on, it gets better." Hans winked.

He waited while the business shots made their way around the table then he brought out the first of the formal shots, the pictures of Emily in the red evening gown. He had printed several shots of her--one that seemed to catch her entering a ballroom; another, a playful shot of her twirling around with her skirt floating like a chiffon cloud around her legs; and last, a shot of her sitting at a table looking expectantly at the door, waiting for someone to arrive with a yearning little smile on her face, and a long stemmed red rose in her hand.

He had only printed one shot of her in the second evening gown but it was the most spectacular shot so far. The gown was a soft shimmering cloud; it had a silver beaded bodice with thin spaghetti straps, and a skirt that was a swirl of tangerine chiffon. There was a very long matching chiffon scarf draped around her neck, the ends fluttering from the force of a strategically placed fan in the studio. Her hair was perfection, a riot of windblown curls.

The pose had her standing against what appeared to be the rail of an ocean liner; the setting seemed to be soaked in moonlight and stars with a gentle breeze in the air. The ship's rails hid many of her figure flaws, and the way she was leaning slightly forward holding the rail emphasized her full breasts. Her expression was filled with tenderness and poignancy. "Hans, I'm speechless," Emily said.

Everyone at the table looked at the picture in awe. It was one of those rare shots that seem to be too good to be of a real human being.

"I hate to break the spell," Hans said finally, "but do you want to see the other shots, Emily?"

"What other shots?" Emily asked, then she blushed. "Oh, those . . . What the heck, bring them out."

She turned to her father and said, "We also shot a few lingerie shots, Dad. Hans is being tactful."

"Hans, I've seen her in lingerie and underwear all her life." Pete grinned. "Fathers do that sometimes when they have daughters running around the house."

The shots were stunning, even if the setting was fairly predictable: a king-sized bed covered with silk sheets and surrounded by thin, wispy curtains. The final shot was the one of the gown as it seemed to hang for a moment, suspended in time, before hitting the floor. The shots were tastefully done, sexy and erotic, but without any nudity. Emily was stunned.

"Wait until David sees these!" Nicole exclaimed.

"I'm not going to show them to David just yet. These will have to wait," Emily said firmly.

"But not too long." Nicole grinned. "As for the rest of these, can I show them to my agent?"

"Sure." Emily grinned. "Why not? She'll either love them or hate them, and the funny thing is, it doesn't matter to me. I love them. You were right, Nicole. These pictures have given me a new confidence."

"I have a separate set of prints for your agents, and duplicate of the proof sheets." Hans rose from his chair and pulled them out of his briefcase. "I'd better go, Emily. Thanks for dinner."

"Thank you, Hans." Emily kissed his cheek and said, "I don't know how to repay you."

"Someday, maybe when you're famous, you will." He smiled at her with genuine friendship. "But for now, your smile is enough."

After Hans left and Nicole followed shortly thereafter, Emily checked her email and found Nicole's basic plan:

BASIC DIET AND FITNESS PLAN:

1. DIET:
A. FIND ONE FOOD OR EVEN MORE (IDEALLY AT LEAST TWO FOODS) THAT YOU CAN ELIMINATE FROM YOUR DIET FOREVER AND ADD AT LEAST TWO HEALTY FOODS.
B. WRITE DOWN EVERYTHING THAT YOU INTEND TO EAT BEFORE YOU EAT IT.
C. MAKE SURE TO EAT VEGATABLES, FRUITS, AND GRAINS AND CLEAR SOUPS FIRST, WATCH OUT FOR CONDIMENTS; QUIT EATING WHEN YOU FEEL FULL.
D. ALLOW YOURSELF A DESSERT ONCE A WEEK. MAKE ALL YOUR OTHER TREATS TO YOURSELF SOMETHING OTHER THAN FOOD.
E. DON'T WEIGH OR MEASURE YOURSELF TOO OFTEN, MAYBE USE MEASUREMENTS INSTEAD OF WEIGHT TO MEASURE YOUR PROGRESS.
F. DRINK LOTS OF WATER.

2. EXERCISE:
A. IF NOTHING ELSE TAKE A WALK EVERY DAY, BUILDING UP BOTH SPEED AND DISTANCE, OR USE A TREADMILL.
B. WORK OUT ON STRENGHTH, TRY USING WEIGHT MACHINES TO BUILD MUSCLE.

C. FIND MORE PHYSICAL HOBBIES--SWIMMING, HORSEBACK RIDING: WHATEVER YOU ENJOY.

3. WARNING:
HAVE A DOCTOR CHECK YOU OUT BEFORE BEGINNING ANY DIET OR EXERCISE PROGRAM.

Reading it over, Emily decided to give it a real try. She found a notepad, then starting making notes about exercise, and foods she could give up. Going slightly against Nicole's advice, she made up a list of goals paired with things she would like to use as rewards for reaching each one of them. She put the notepad in her purse.

She made a note to show the plan to the doctor next time she took her father in for a visit. Her father's doctor was always offering to give her a quick check-up and to answer her questions. He took his time with her, and he was patient with Mae. Emily thought he was one of the best men she knew.

Chapter Eleven

Two days later, David showed up bright and early on her doorstep. Totally ignoring her parents he enfolded her into his arms in a warm hug, accompanied by a tender but passionate kiss.

"It seemed like I'd never get home." He grinned, kissing her again.

"I missed you, too." Emily smiled at him with a trace of the devil in her smile. "But I was busy while you were gone."

"You better not have been busy with another guy." He was only partly teasing.

"Silly man, are there even any other guys around? I can't see 'em." She reveled in the warmth of his arms. "I spent a lot of time with Nicole."

"You did?" David's eyebrow's shot up. "What did you two get up to?"

Emily still wanted to surprise David with her riding, so she just shrugged. "Well, we ah, worked out in the gym and went swimming. We also did a makeover and photo shoot."

"I can tell." He looked her over. "Your hair looks fantastic, and if I'm any judge of it, you've lost some weight."

"Just a little." Emily smiled at him, snuggling in his arms.

"More than a little, I'd bet." He kissed her forehead, smiling.

"Will you have dinner with me tonight?" David asked.

"Sure." She grinned. "I've got nothing better to do."

"You'd better not have," David growled, then he looked at his watch. "Oh man! I've got to run. I'm due in court in twenty minutes. I don't want the judge to fine me for contempt."

"Then get going!" Emily laughed as she gave him a gentle shove. "See you tonight," Emily added.

That night over dinner she gave David a surprise. She showed him the photos Hans had shot. David loved them. He was shocked to see how relaxed Emily looked in the casual scene, how natural she looked in the office scene, but it was the formal pictures that really blew him away; she looked sexy and confident, and very desirable. She gave him an 8 x 10 of the picture of her in the tangerine and silver gown. She held something back however, she didn't bring out any of the lingerie photos to show him.

For the rest of the week, they were together every evening. They went out to dinner on Thursday, but the rest of the week they spent at Emily's with her folks.

While they were at dinner, David told Emily about an idea that he'd had. It was an idea that seemed too outrageous to be real, but the more Emily examined it, the more she admitted it could work. His idea was deceptively simple: She could have Julia move in with her family and be there to work part time as a private care nurse for her folks.

"I've talked to her, even before I met you and she said the property taxes are eating her alive. She has someone who wants to buy her place. Actually," he admitted, "I want to buy most of her land, and someone else wants the part with her house on it. I took the liberty of asking her if she'd be interested, and she said she would. She doesn't even want a salary, just room and board. She only wants to care for your folks part time because she wants to have time for herself, but even so it'd be a bargain for you. I know she'd be there when you needed her. It's good for her, too. If she moved in with you, she wouldn't have to spend the money she gets from the sale of her land for living expenses. She can save it so she'll have enough money for her future. She'll find a new place when you, I'm sorry, no longer need her services."

"Let me think it over but it sounds like a good idea. She's very good with both of my folks. She's patient with my mom, and she treats my dad with kindness and respect. She doesn't baby him like so many people seem to do." Emily mused aloud, "It would sure free me up to get out of the house more, maybe even work a little. Nicole said her agent is interested in my photos. In fact, she sold the picture I gave you to a catalog, and one that I haven't shown you yet to a calendar."

"There's some you haven't shown me?" David picked up on it immediately. "Why not? When can I see them?"

"I'm saving them for the right moment, and that's all I will say about them for now." Emily smiled mysteriously.

That Saturday they finally spent the day at David's house with her parents. David told her to come around noon since he had the vet coming out to give the horses some shots and a check-up before she got there.

David used the time alone with the vet to ask him if he knew of any dogs that wouldn't cause Pete's allergies to act up.

"We can give him some antihistamines for today and see how it goes," David explained to the vet. "His doctor said it was okay for a special occasion, but still it would be nice if we could find a dog that he could live with. Emily would really love a puppy and I thought I'd get her one for her birthday."

"I'd check with the doctor but I think a hairless dog would be okay." She smiled as she loaded her supplies into her vet truck. "I know of a litter of Chinese Crested puppies that are ready for new homes in about a week, call my office for the number."

When Emily pulled up with her folks, David had just watched the vet drive away. She got her folks out and set them up in some chairs in the shade not too far from the arena. True to her doctor's prediction, Mae remembered very well how to act around horses and how to ride. In fact, she thought it had only been a few days since her last ride! She fell in love with Target, calling him "Brownie" and refused to use a saddle, preferring to ride him with just a halter and rope. Target plodded around the arena, some equine instinct telling the big horse to be careful. David rode Nicole's horse, and to his surprise, Emily rode his young horse.

That was the subject of some discussion, almost a fight, when David realized that Emily was riding almost daily with Nicole, and the young horse which they just called junior, was her usual mount.

"I didn't know you'd be upset that I was riding Junior," Emily explained after she had Junior out and saddled. "Nicole said it would be okay."

"She should have known better, or at least asked me," David grumbled. "But you haven't been hurt, so I guess it's okay. Anyway, it wasn't your fault so I shouldn't be mad at you."

"Are you worried that this horse is going to hurt me? Is he mean?" Emily was incredulous as she mounted. "He's been very good with me!"

"Yes, I would have been a little worried, but Nicole is a good rider and she would know how to teach you. Don't get me wrong, Junior's not a bit mean, he's very good-hearted, but he's also very green." David smiled into Emily's eyes. "That means he's not very well trained, and he may be a little unpredictable. You say you haven't had any trouble with him?"

"No," Emily grinned, patting his neck, "he's as gentle as a kitten. A very big kitten." Junior was about eleven hundred pounds.

"What have you been doing with him? Riding in the arena or trail riding?" David asked.

"Mostly riding in the arena, we work along the rail then I watch Nicole work her horse and then I copy her, only much slower." Emily grinned.

"Copy her?" David's voice rose slightly.

"I ride the same patterns around the poles and barrels that she does only, like I said before, much slower." Emily looked defiant and a little hurt. "Is there a problem with that?"

"I'll let you know after I see you ride him around those same patterns." David smiled. "But please understand this: if there's a problem, it's Nicole's problem, not yours. In the meantime, why don't you help me pick out a new name for Junior?"

"Nicole said he already has a registered name, Midnight Raider," Emily ventured.

"True, I'd hate to go around calling him Midnight. It's just not the right name for a sorrel horse, and if I call him Raider I'd wind up being Raider's rider, and that sounds tacky." David grinned. "Of course as long as you're riding him, you'll be Raider's rider."

"I'd be proud." Emily grinned, thrilled. "I'd be proud to be Raider's rider."

"So, Raider's rider, run the pole bending pattern for me," David commanded.

He watched as she ran the first of the four courses that he had marked out so that they could be set up easily in the larger arena. It was called pole bending, and Nicole had left it up the last time they'd ridden. The course consisted of a row of six poles spaced twenty feet apart. All the rider had to do in this variation was weave through the poles up and back. Emily trotted the horse through the pole bending course, then she gathered her courage and went through the course again, this time at a gentle lope.

"So," David asked, "when do you run him?"

"That wasn't a run?" Emily asked.

"No, that was a lope." David laughed even as he instructed her. "Try it again, only faster. I'll time you."

Emily pushed the big horse through the course again, this time quite a bit faster. David turned on the electric timer.

"How did I do?" Emily asked.

"Really well. You looked smooth and he was just skimming the poles, not wasting any movement. Your time was 16.5 seconds, which is just about right for a practice session at this stage of his training. Now I'm going to take Nicole's horse through."

He ran the course on Nicole's horse in a decent time of 10.2. Emily was amazed that he was so much faster than she was.

"I took almost twice as long as you did, and I thought I was going so fast." Emily was slightly put out. "How do I get him up to speed?"

"The same way you get to Carnegie Hall." David grinned.

Emily thought for a while before she remembered the old line, "Practice, practice, practice?"

"You've got it," David told her. "And I think you're getting good enough to skip the trot through and the slow lope, just go for the half speed run like you did today, unless he starts giving you a problem. Time yourself and don't try to beat me or Nicole, try to beat yourself. You've set a time of 16.5, so aim to beat that next time. Just don't push him too hard here at home, work on keeping him calm and relaxed, under control, okay?"

"You mean I get to keep riding him?" Emily's eyes glowed.

"Sweetheart, as far as I'm concerned he's all yours." He leaned over to kiss her, then he jumped off and handed her the reins. "Let's practice quadrangle."

"I don't know that one very well," Emily admitted, watching David move the poles using green markings that he had painted on his arena fence as guides for placing them.

Pete walked over to watch too. "Are you okay, Daddy? Is this too tiring for you?" Emily asked. "Are your allergies acting up?"

"No, I'm fine, Sweetheart. That new antihistamine the doctor gave me seems to be working," Pete told her. "In fact, I was going to ask David if I could help him with the tape measure."

Pete ducked through the fence and walked over to David. Soon he was indeed helping David measure the course, which consisted mainly of a seventy-five foot square, with two timing poles twenty feet apart in the center. The practice session went well although Emily was right, neither she nor Raider were very familiar with Quad. After that, David set up the barrel race, the most well known and basic gymkhana event while Emily went over and got her mother off Target and put him away.

"Did you enjoy your ride, Mom?" she asked.

"Of course, I always enjoy riding Brownie," her mom replied. "I am a little stiff though. I think I'll go sit down." She went over to sit near Pete on one of the folding chairs David had placed next to the arena.

David and Emily went through the barrel course one time each. Emily was several seconds slower than David.

"How on earth does it feel to go as fast as you do?" Emily asked, gasping. "Even at this speed I feel like I'm flying."

"There's a way I can show you but it's probably a little dangerous. Are you game?" David challenged.

"Sure." Emily's chin went up. "What do I do?"

"Follow me as close as you can, we're going to do what we call fox and hounds, which is a sort of a follow-the-leader barrel race. First we'll trot through, then lope, then half speed. Lastly, if your horse seems to have a clue as to what's going on, we'll run it. You'll have to be careful to avoid having a collision with me, so it's best if you stay as close as possible. Think you can do it?" he asked.

"I think so, we'll see how it goes at the slower speeds." Emily was determined.

At the slower speeds everything was smooth. David felt like Raider had the idea of what was going on so they talked it over and agreed to try it at almost full speed.

"Stay as close to me as you can," David instructed. "And stay alert, we don't want any accidents."

The ride went well in spite of the fact that Raider tried his equine best to beat the more experienced horse David was on, instead of being content to follow behind. The best time Emily had run on her own was 26.4 so she was amazed when the exhilarating ride ended to find out that their combined time, from the time David crossed the starting line until Emily crossed the finish line was 20.1.

She steadied Raider who was now prancing and tossing his head. "Wow! That felt wonderful!"

"Do you think you could be my partner at a horse show?" David asked, grinning widely.

"Me? Really? I'm nowhere near experienced enough." Emily smiled back softly. "But thanks for asking."

"Emily, my love, I wouldn't ask you if you weren't good enough. I can't believe how far you've come in such a short time." David reached out and almost pulled her off Raider, kissing her firmly. "So will you?"

"Yes." She was mesmerized by his use of the phrase "my love" but she managed to kiss him back before Raider danced away.

Chapter Twelve

"Whoa, boy." She patted the big horse tenderly, calming him and praising him.

"That was great, Emily! I can't believe how good a rider you've become in such a short time!" her father called out. "You're fantastic!"

"Thanks, Daddy." She beamed.

"Let's skip speed barrels; I think these two have had enough. We can put them on the hot walker and have a cold drink while they cool off," David suggested.

"Sounds good to me," Emily agreed.

She got off Raider and unsaddled him, putting his saddle in the barn and leaving his blanket to dry off upside down in the sun. She pulled off the horse's headstall and rubbed his head, scratching all of the places where he had gotten a little sweaty under his bridle. She haltered him then watched while David hosed off both horses and used a sweat scraper to remove most of the water. He put the horses on the hot walker.

The hot walker had a center pole with four arms radiating out form it, and at the end of each arm was a chain hanging down with a snap at the end. David snapped each horse to an arm and turned on the hot walker so that the center pole turned slowly causing each horse to walk in a small circle. The hot walker could be used to cool off a hot horse after a workout or to keep a horse moving until he dried off after a bath.

Emily went in and showered quickly then walked into the kitchen to get some iced tea and lemonade. When she got back outside she found that her parents and David had moved up to sit at the patio table. As soon as they had all gotten comfortable and Emily had served everyone with their choice of tea or lemonade, Nicole arrived.

"Hi everyone, how was the ride?" Nicole breezed in.

"We had a great time as soon as I got over the shock of finding out that Emily here was riding my green horse through gymkhana courses," David said with a trace of steel in his voice.

"Oops!" Nicole was unrepentant. "I guess I'm in trouble. How did she do?"

"She was great, especially when we ran fox and hounds with," David shot her a look that was pure trouble, "me on your horse."

"You're dead meat, buddy." Her fabulous eyes narrowed.

"Right after you, sister dear." His tone was deceptively mild.

"I think I'll go in and get things ready for dinner." Emily decided that cowardice was the better part of valor.

"I'll feed your folks while David finishes taking care of the horses." Nicole smiled, stopping Emily's retreat into the house. "Don't worry, we won't kill each other."

David went to the barn and fed Target. He also put hay and grain into the stalls for Raider and Nick's horse, checked the water for all three horses, and made sure the stalls were clean. He turned off the hot walker and both horses instantly peed, as if they'd been fighting the urge for hours, but he knew it was only a form of equine protest. He unsnapped Nicole's horse and gave him a slap on the hindquarters. The horse headed straight for his stall. He unsnapped Raider and led him into the barn. He removed the horses' halters before making sure all three stall doors were tightly shut.

Soon David and Emily were on their way to dinner while Nicole fed her parents and took them home.

Over dinner Emily started a conversation. "David, how do you keep your horses so well mannered when so many of the horses I saw at the horse show were so high strung?"

"I believe that even a gymkhana horse should be a pleasure to ride so I put a lot of effort into training them to have manners, and I try to differentiate between times when they're going to be asked to run and everyday rides by changing both my equipment and my attitude. Also, I don't run them all out every time I get on them. Once they know an event I just practice enough to keep it in their minds, and I seldom run full out at home, even if it looks like I did today. I ran Nicole's horse but I didn't push her. See the difference?"

"I see, and I think you're right. At the horse show it seemed like some of the kids were speed freaks like their horses." Emily smiled. "It's okay for them, but I like your way better."

The waitress brought their dinners and they dropped the conversation to eat. Sitting there over the empty plates, having a last glass of iced tea, Emily asked another question that was bothering her.

"Why is Nicole so concerned about overweight people?" Emily asked. "Her concern is great but a little unusual, especially for a model. Most people who are in terrific shape seem to look at heavy people as if they were seeing their worst nightmare."

"Ask her. I think she'll tell you," David replied. "It's tied in to her reasons for wanting to quit modeling. I'm glad she's helping you, though."

"I'm glad for her help, of course. It's good to have a friend like Nicole. I do have a big question, though." She paused, hesitating before she asked, "If I go all out with the diet and exercise how will it affect our relationship?"

"What do you mean?" David was puzzled.

"A lot of times when someone who's as heavy as I am goes on a diet, people around her feel threatened. They wind up trying to sabotage the diet. Some men even have a special attraction for large women. In fact, for one of those men, I'd be considered too skinny." Emily grimaced. "Can you believe it?"

"Emily, you really hurt my feelings. You should know by now that I'll support you whether you go on a diet or not. I'll be here whether your diet is successful or not. I want to be with you more and more as time passes and I suspect that this feeling is only going to get stronger. I already want to make love with you."

"David, I'm sorry. I always seem to be taking my own insecurities out on you. You're very important to me and having someone like you in my life is very new to me." She reached out and covered his hand with hers. "As for making love, I'm not quite ready yet, and my beliefs, well. . . It's as sin."

"I know, I believe that too," David said with some regret, "but I do want to make love with you."

"But I do know you want me and I realize that you accept me as I am, really I do, but I don't quite accept myself. At least not entirely."

"Are you saying that you won't really love me until you reach some weight goal? Or hit a certain dress size?" David's eyes blazed. "That's crazy! I don't want to wait that long!"

"I'm glad you're not willing to wait that long, neither am I. I'm just a little hesitant about my body, and I'm new to this love business." She stroked his hand. "Please be patient."

"Okay. But please, try to get over your fears as soon as you can. I'm trying to be patient, but it's all an act." David grinned. "Right or wrong, sin or not, I'm as impatient as hell."

"I wouldn't want to take advantage of your patience." Emily grinned. "I just want to take advantage of your body, when it's right. And soon, I will be ready soon, I promise."

They took a short drive after dinner, mainly to be alone. Finally, parked on a road out in the country, David took her into his arms and made a powerful argument in favor of red hot passion.

Over the next three weeks they had more dates, more rides, and more quiet times spent in each other's arms. Luckily, her father seemed to be holding his own. One day, David came over when Emily was out shopping and he had a long, quiet discussion with Pete.

"Pete, I want to talk to you about Emily when she's not

around," he began. "I want you to know that I really care for her, heck, I love her. It's not just . . ."

"I know, I can see it when I see you together," Pete said softly, "but I don't think Emily realizes it, not really. She's got so much on her mind. I've been praying that I could see her in love, see the man who would love her, before I died."

David was too wise to deny Pete's illness. "I'd like to have you at our wedding, but I don't think Emily's ready for that yet."

"I'd love to be there to walk her down the aisle, to see her married and in love. It would be the answer to my prayers," Pete said, smiling sadly. "I'll admit, I was losing hope before she met you; I'm learning that prayers and faith work miracles. Whether I'm at the wedding or not, I've had a burden lifted from my mind now that you're in her life. It makes it easier on me."

"Pete? Emily's birthday is Saturday, right?" David fought to hide tears.

"It is." Pete smiled. "You have something up you sleeve, I can see it in your eyes. So what have you got in mind to surprise her with?"

"I have an idea." David walked over closer to Pete. "I know she wants a puppy and I know that you have allergies. I talked to my vet and she suggested I talk to your doctor and see if it would be safe, for you, to get her a hairless puppy. She even knows of a Chinese Crested puppy that would be ready for her new home on Emily's birthday."

"Are those the dogs that are so ugly they're cute?" Pete laughed a bit. "That's a great idea. Emily would love that."

"And one more thing." David paused. "The next weekend I'm taking the horses to Santa Barbara for a horse show. I'd like to take Emily."

"I'd like that, she needs to get away," Pete said slowly.

"Not for sex, you understand," David told him. "And we always have an informal Church service on the show grounds for those who want to attend."

"That's good," Pete added.

"I want to surprise her and enter her on Raider." David asked, "What do you think?"

"I just wish I could be there." The older man seemed to grow frailer by the moment. "Just like I'd like to be at your wedding."

"I'll do what I can." David looked Pete in the eyes. "I promise."

When David left, Pete seemed more cheerful and relaxed than he had in a long time.

The next night as David and Emily bobbed in the hot tub, David brought up her birthday and asked her what she wanted. He didn't mention the puppy he had already bought. They bobbed in the water and talked softly.

"I already have one present for you," David leaned over to kiss her, "but I wanted to ask you if you would accept more."

"I love presents, but I figured just having you in my life was my present this year." She grinned and reached out to tickle his ribs. "What'd you get me?"

"I'm not telling." He laughed. "Even if you torture me."

"How about if I kiss it out of you?" She moved closer.

"My lips are sealed," he managed before her mouth closed over his.

Emily put a lot of effort into unsealing his lips, but he wouldn't give up his secret.

"Well, if that didn't do it, I'm stumped." Emily pouted.

"You'll just have to wait for your birthday," David said smugly.

That night when David took her home they sat in his car talking in front of her house.

"I want to ask you something," David said hesitantly for once. "I'm going to a horse show in Santa Barbara next weekend. I'm leaving Friday morning and driving back Sunday night."

He paused.

"You want me to watch the horses?" Emily guessed. "Sure.

I'd love to."

"That's not it. Nicole's putting her horse in a boarding stable for a few days since she's going to be out of town on assignment for a while. I'm taking Target and Raider, so there won't be any horses to watch. Kate and Bob will watch the dogs."

"Then what is it?" Emily's pulse was racing now.

"I want you to come with me." David had a pleading look in his eyes.

"I can't, David. My parents . . ." Emily was regretful.

"Julia's there now. She'll call us if there's a crises and I'll take you home on the first flight we can catch and go back for the horses later. You need to get away." David looked at her tenderly then continued, "I'll make sure you have your own room. I'll book a suite with two bedrooms, whatever you want."

"It sounds fun, more than fun. I want to go." Emily thought for a moment then said, "Let me think about it, okay?"

"I should tell you, don't be mad, but I asked your father if it would be okay with him if I took you away for the weekend, next weekend." David paused. "He seemed to think it was great."

"I bet you didn't mention hotel rooms to him," Emily muttered.

"You win that bet, I'm not stupid." David grinned at her. "Going?"

"Yes. I will." Suddenly everything seemed so clear to Emily, she would go on the weekend with David and stay in touch with Julia on her cell phone.

She smiled to herself and said, "I'm mature enough and secure enough in my faith to resist temptation. I hope."

For the most part Emily had faith in David, in their future together, and in their love for each other. Emily still had some of her insecurities though, and they surfaced from time to time. She still had low self-esteem. Sometimes she still thought of herself as a fat slob, even though she had lost just over forty pounds. She even worried that David might get tired of dealing with her problems. David was patient but the need to constantly reassure Emily so often was getting on his nerves.

One night David called Emily from his office and cancelled their dinner date, saying he had to work late. She considered staying home and watching TV but instead she decided to take Pete, Mae and Julia out to dinner. She got Mae dressed up nicely, helped Pete get ready, and took the group to one of the nicer restaurants in town. They were halfway through dinner when David walked in with one of the most beautiful women Emily had ever seen. She was tall, blonde, and beautifully built.

One look at David, sitting there with this woman, talking with her, laughing with her, seemed to crystallize all of Emily's worst fears. What if the warmth and loving he showed her was just an act? What if he was tired of her? She thought back and realized he had been working late a lot more recently.

Stop it! Emily told herself, David had been working harder than usual to catch up on things that he'd let slide since they'd met. He loved her and constantly let her know it. Excusing herself, Emily went into the ladies room, mainly to compose herself. She freshened her make-up, straightened her clothes, and brushed out her long hair. She was just about to leave the ladies room when David's date came in and began fussing with her make-up.

"I saw you out there, having dinner with David Silvan," Emily ventured.

"You know David?" The woman laughed lightly. "Isn't he about the sexiest man you ever met?"

At Emily's nod she continued, "I usually let men pursue me but for a hunk like him, I'll make an exception."

"I'd wish you luck, but he's taken," Emily said with a trace of defiance.

"So what? There aren't many women who can compete with me," the other woman shot back, smiling into the mirror.

"I'm sure there aren't." Emily turned to leave the room,

shaken inside.

She walked over to David's table and said, "Hi David."

"Emily!" David got up. "It's so good to see you! I thought I'd be tied up with my client all evening."

He hugged and kissed her warmly.

"I'm here with Mom and Dad, and Julia." She gestured across the room. "I saw you here with someone so I decided to come over and say hello."

"Stay here and meet Megan, my new client. I'm going over a major contract with her. She's one of the top models in the world." David watched Emily closely for signs that her low self-esteem had resurfaced.

"I talked to her in the ladies room," Emily said. "She mentioned wanting more than legal services from you."

"What did you say?" he quizzed her.

"I told her you were taken," Emily replied, her chin held high.

"In other words, you told her the truth." David grinned. "Because I am taken, by you." He kissed her. "Why don't I come over when I'm through here?"

"You'd better." Emily turned to go back to her table and almost bumped into the beautiful Megan.

"Have a great dinner. Nice meeting you, Megan," Emily said as she turned to leave.

"Nice meeting you. . ." Megan floundered.

"Emily," David supplied.

"Nice meeting you, Emily." Megan held out her hand, with a warm smile on her face.

"Same here. I'd better get back to my table." Emily shook Megan's hand and then left.

"Your um. . . friend seems very nice, David," Megan said, sitting down and grinning ruefully. "Is it serious?"

David nodded and smiled the biggest smile Megan had ever seen. "She doesn't know it yet, but she's going to be my wife."

"She's made you happy, I can tell." Megan reached for a roll.

"I'm a little surprised that you weren't taken by one of Nikki's model friends, though."

"Actually, Emily *is* doing some modeling for full figure fashions. I guess I see enough glamorous women to see that most of you are really just ordinary people with great looks. Some models are vain, some models are air heads, and some, most, are warm, intelligent women." David smiled at a memory. "It was a surprise when I met Emily though. We were at a horse show and she was scared of the horses, and dirty. She weighed more than she does now."

"Really?" Megan was interested in the story.

"Sure, Nicole's been working with her to teach her fashion sense, and how to use make-up. It doesn't matter to me, except for Emily's sake, for her self-confidence." David smiled softly. "I enjoyed talking to her most of the day at that horse show and then, when I took a fall, she ran over to see how I was and I looked up into her face and fell hard."

"David, I think you made a good choice," Megan said with a trace of regret in her voice.

"Trust me Megan, I didn't choose to fall in love, it chose me," David told her.

A few nights later when a quiet dinner at David's had turned into tender loving, David told her about Megan's comment.

"She's sometimes vain and she can be ruthless about getting what she wants, so I'm a little surprised that she gave up so easily." David smiled. "She must have known it was really a hopeless case."

Emily just smiled.

Emily's birthday was great. Aside from the puppy, Pete and Mae gave her a laptop, and Nicole had sent some new clothes and all the supplies for her new puppy she would need. Her friends Kate and Laura and their husbands came over with their kids. Even Kate's friend Frank brought his family. Emily wound up with a pile of gifts and a great cake.

When Frank learned Emily was working with David's young horse he suggested, "Why don't you come over and ride with my daughter a few times. She doesn't ride gymkhana events, she does Western Equitation. It would give you a chance to learn about more events."

"That's a great idea!" David reached over and picked up the puppy. "You can learn more about the different events and see if you like something other than gymkhana."

Later, David took Emily aside away from the group. "Emily, there's one more thing I want to give you." He paused, suddenly nervous. "I know we haven't been together long, but I know what I feel. I love you, Emily, and I want to marry you."

He pulled out a ring.

"This is pretty quick, but it feels right. Let me ask you one thing: Are you doing this so fast because of my father?" She met his eyes.

"Partly, but it's what I want, too," he admitted, "more than anything."

"That's so thoughtful." Emily sighed. "I want you to understand, I don't want to get married just to make my father happy, I want to get married because I love you. I think you're my miracle."

He put the ring on Emily's finger and together they went in and told their friends.

David pulled Kate's husband Bob aside and said, "I seem to recall that you know a lot about planning a wedding."

Bob had surprised Kate with a wedding in the disguise of a family reunion.

"I need help to get this planned as quickly as possible."

Bob looked over at Pete and then turned back to David. "You've got it, anything I can do."

"Thanks."

The week passed in a blur, with Emily getting ready for the weekend trip. Still the time passed slowly because David had to work late several nights to get the weekend off. David was also on the phone a lot, calling the caterers, photographers, and the wedding cake maker that Bob suggested.

Emily called David and asked, "What should I pack?"

"Well, wear something comfortable to travel in, and take two sets of clothes to run around the horse show. Let's see, you should take a nice Western shirt for each day, and also a grubby t-shirt for each day. You'll need something to go out to dinner in a nice restaurant, for both nights, and something to swim in. That should be it."

"How about something to sleep in?" Emily asked flirtatiously.

"You'll have plenty to sleep in. You can sleep in my hotel room, even in my bed, and in my arms if you want," David replied in kind.

"David, dear. You know I can't do that, my conscious won't let me." She let the words hang in the air.

"We're mature enough not to cross any lines," David said slowly. "We can just cuddle.

"If I decide to spend the weekend in your room, your bed, and your arms, I wouldn't get any sleep and neither would you." She hung up.

Chapter Thirteen

That Friday morning Emily drove over to David's and parked her car. She pulled her luggage out of the trunk and sat it next to David's truck which was already hooked up to a horse trailer. With the puppy she'd named Top Knot, for the small tuft of hair that stuck up between his ears, on a leash, she walked into the barn to find David wrapping Target's legs.

"Is that to protect them while they travel or what?" she asked, watching him work.

"You're very quick. Yes, it's for protection. I usually don't bother when I take Target to a local show, but for a five hour drive, even he will get restless." David looked up at her. "You look great!"

"Thanks, David." She grinned. "Really, it's just a pair of shorts and a T-shirt. I took your advice and went for comfort."

"You can put your bags in the truck if you want." He finished the leg he was working on before he stood up and kissed her. He knelt again to work on Target's other front leg.

She threw her bags into the truck as he suggested. It seemed like a lot for only two nights, but she'd only packed what he'd suggested. Clothes to care for the horses in, and nice clothes for the show, plus two dresses to go out to eat in, and she also included make-up.

David finished wrapping Target's legs and asked Emily to walk him around while he started on Raider. She tied Top Knot's leash to a tree and started to lead Target around. The big horse walked so funny, raising each leg so high and shaking it, that Emily laughed.

"What's he doing?" she asked David. "Has he gone nuts?"

"He's getting the feel for the bandages," David told her. "I don't use them very often. Wait 'til you see how Raider acts."

In a short time, Target calmed down and began to walk more normally. She tied him to the side of the trailer. David finished Raider and Emily walked him. True to David's prediction, Raider's walk was even more exaggerated and it took him longer to settle down. Meanwhile, David loaded Target into the trailer.

Emily brought Raider over to David as soon as he began to settle down. Raider was not as good a traveler as Target, so when David loaded him, he had Emily stand behind the horse, but safely off to one side.

"Watch him, in case he spooks," David instructed her, "but click to him and pat his rump to ask him to go in. Be careful."

Raider went in more reluctantly than Target, but he was calm enough. David made sure each horse was fastened in place before shutting the trailer door.

He turned to Emily. "I just want to say that I'm so excited and glad you're coming with me."

"I'm glad I'm going." Emily smiled back at him, trying to suppress her excitement and nerves.

She watched as he went around the truck to the passenger side and opened the door for her. She untied the puppy and got into the car.

"Let's hit the road!" David pulled the rig out of his long driveway and onto the country road.

It was a great day for the trip, warm but not hot. The traffic was still light as they had avoided most of the weekend crush. The horses were well behaved and the scenery was fantastic. Emily and David talked about everything. Only two topics were left off the table, by unspoken consent. One was whether or not they'd sleep together that night, and the other was her father's health. She made sure Julia had David's number on speed dial, and that was it. Of course, they did discuss their upcoming wedding. David told her about the help he'd gotten from Bob,

"Because he put together his own surprise wedding?" she asked.

"Yes, and in a very short time," David said. "Ours is kind of different. Emily, we may need to move up the date and location, but God willing, it's going to be great."

"It's an answer to my prayers that I'm marrying you at all, I can get married anytime and anywhere." She looked at him with tenderness in her eyes. "It would only take one thing to make it perfect."

"I know my love, I know." He reached over to grasp her hand.

After about three hours they stopped at a hamburger stand for lunch. They watered the horses and ate their burgers, sitting by the trailer. Some of the kids whose families were eating there came over to look into the trailer and see the horses. They also fell in love with the puppy who ate up the attention as if it was her due. Since David was used to this reaction to his horses, he had some carrots ready for the kids to give the horses as they stuck their noses out the side window. He was careful to ask the parents on hand for permission before letting any of the children feed the horses.

When there was a break in the line of children they got back into the truck and started up again. They pulled into Santa Barbara around 4 PM, and then made their way to the show grounds. David stopped and got the stall numbers for the horses, then pulled them around to their barn.

He unloaded both horses, handing Raider off to Emily before he got Target out. Emily took a hint from him and unwrapped Raider's legs. Then she walked him around for a few minutes before tying him to a rail in front of the barn. David did the same with Target.

Together they broke open a bale of straw and spread it in each stall. David had hooks to hang the hay sacks, water buckets, and grain buckets. He fastened the buckets and then filled each one, using a hose he'd brought for the water. They let the horses into the stalls.

Next he began the long process of unloading the trailer. First was a toolbox filled with eyebolts and a screwdriver. He put up several hooks in the tack room.

"Don't they complain about you putting holes is the walls?" Emily wondered.

"Nope." David explained, "Look at these walls."

Emily realized that the walls were indeed covered with hooks and holes from old hooks.

"I try to use the old hooks and holes as much as possible," David said, "but this is how things are done."

They unloaded their tack, David's show clothes, and the other supplies they had. Some of the things they hung on the hooks. They had barrels for the grain, and the hay was put outside by the horses' stalls. They had a lot of things for each horse: a halter and lead, a blanket, a saddle and bridle with saddle pad, and a set of brushes for each horse. They also had first aid supplies for horses and people, some folding chairs, a radio and a cooler. David also brought out some hat boxes and some garment bags which he hung on a nail on the wall. He set up the puppy's bed in the corner, and arranged a barricade across the doorway to prevent any chance of escape. He also had a small, but sturdy cot.

"If we were roughing it, I would have brought something for us both to sleep on and a small rug to cover this cement floor." David squeezed her. "I, for one, am glad we have hotel rooms."

"Me too, although staying here could be fun if I were with you." Emily snuggled in his arms.

"Emily, I think that's the nicest thing you've ever said to me." David kissed her. "Let's go unhitch the trailer and check in to the hotel."

"Sounds good to me, I want a shower. I feel grubby." Emily grinned. "And I wouldn't mind some food."

They found the parking area and unhitched the trailer.

They were pulling into the hotel parking structure when Emily finally spoke up. "David, I'd better warn you. I made some changes to your reservations."

"What'd you do? Call them and ask for completely separate rooms, maybe on separate floors?" David asked with a touch of exasperation in his voice. "Don't you trust me?"

"No, you big dope. I cancelled that extra bed. I know we can't make love yet but I wanted to sleep with you and just cuddle so we won't be needing it," Emily grinned, "unless you want to sleep alone?"

"So? You've decided we don't need to sleep at all, because I sure will have trouble just sleeping with you in my arms. I love the idea, thank heavens, who needs sleep?" He parked and took her into his arms. "I love you, Emily."

He kissed her until she pulled away.

"Let's go find our room and a shower before we get too carried away in the parking garage." Emily smiled up at the tenderness in his expression. "And, David, I love you, too." Arm in arm, they walked inside the hotel.

As soon as they were in the room, after the bellboy had been tipped and left, they stood facing each other, the air filled with electricity. All of a sudden the bedroom door seemed to be only the thing in the sitting room.

Finally David said softly, "Emily, why don't you take a nice bubble bath and I'll put our clothes away and order something from room service?"

"Are we having dinner here in the room?" she asked.

"We can if you want, or I can just order us something for now. What do you think? Should I order dinner or something like champagne and appetizers?" he asked.

"Champagne sounds good. Why don't you order some and we'll worry about dinner later?" Emily suggested.

"Okay," David kissed her forehead gently, "you go take a nice bath."

Emily took her small bag into the suite's bathroom and gasped aloud. This hotel was known for it's luxurious, almost decadent bathrooms with extra large tubs that were easily big enough for two. Alongside the tub were several small plastic bottles of bubble bath. David walked over to stand in the doorway behind Emily.

"It's wonderful isn't it?" He nuzzled her ear. "It's the main reason I chose this particular hotel."

"It's beautiful, thank you for bringing me here." Emily turned and kissed him. "Now, go away and let me take a nice long bath."

As soon as David left the doorway she closed the door and turned on the water. She adjusted the temperature and began filling the tub. She decided on a bubble bath and emptied it into the stream of running water. While the tub finished filling, she laid out a few of her cosmetics. She took off her clothes, which seemed to be terminally grubby after a day of travel and caring for horses, and put them into a large trash bag that she had brought with her. Then she sank into the hot bubbly water. As soon as she laid back in the tub, resting her head on the end of it, she began to relax. She drifted off for a while then scrubbed herself clean before she emptied and refilled the tub again with hot water and bubbles. Before long, David rapped gently on the door.

"Are you still in the bath?" he asked gently.

"Yes, I'll be out in a minute," she told him.

"Don't hurry," he said softly, "Is the door locked?"

"No." Her voice was soft, almost tremulous.

"Good, sink down into the bubbles, I'm bringing you a glass of champagne." There was a world of determination in his words.

"David! I'm in the tub! I'm naked!" In spite of the desire she felt for David, Emily was alarmed by the idea of him seeing her naked.

"I should hope you're naked. Who takes a bath with their

clothes on?" he teased. "So, cover your eyes. I'm coming in."

"David, it's not my eyes I'm worried about, it's yours," she protested.

"I'll be okay, trust me." He entered the room holding a tray with two glasses of champagne and a bowl of large strawberries. "How's the bath?"

"Wonderful." She felt his eyes roaming all over her body and knew she was beginning to blush. "Warm, and getting warmer by the minute." She took a long sip of champagne and leaned back, her eyes closed, letting David feed her a strawberry. "I should keep you around."

"That's the plan, my love, that's the plan." He leaned over to kiss the champagne from her soft lips.

"I also should get out and let you take your bath. You spent the day traveling and working with horses, too." Her eyes were still closed and she laid back, relaxing.

"I could always join you in the tub," he suggested gently. "After all, it seems like we're going to share more than a bathtub tonight."

Emily's eyes shot open. "That's right. Why didn't I think of that?"

"Maybe you just haven't had enough time to realize that we're going to share a lot of things with each other." David stepped out of the room, returning with the ice bucket and bottle of champagne. "We wouldn't want to run out." He took off his polo shirt. "Is it okay?"

Emily struggled to ignore both the shivers running down her spine and the faint traces of apprehension churning in the pit of her stomach. "As long as it's okay for me to blush a little from time to time."

"Blush all you want too, it's expected of virgins." He unzipped his pants and stepped out of them.

She watched in silent appreciation as he lowered his underwear and stepped out of them. "I'm going to be the one to blush if you keep looking at me like that."

"I'd say I was sorry, but I'm not." She grinned.

"Good." He stepped into the tub facing her. "I want you to enjoy looking at me as much as I enjoy looking at you, and . . ." he continued, his eyes narrowing, "if you even think about making some idiotic remark about your weight, I'll do something violent."

"Like what?" Her chin came up.

"Like this." He moved quickly to cover her, kissing her with a passion that left her breathless while his hands were sliding all over her soapy body, exploring, teasing and arousing her all at once. By the time the kiss was finished, all traces of her insecurities were gone.

All too soon he pulled back with a visible effort, breathing heavily. "Turn around," he managed to say, "I'll wash your hair for you."

She leaned back against his warm body, conscious of the hard flesh of his arousal pressing into her, and let him wash and rinse her hair. Then his hands moved on. She began to moan softly as his soapy fingers stroked and teased her. She let him arouse her, putting herself totally into his hands and soon he had taken her over the brink. She was gasping, rubbing the back of her head against his firm chest as she reached her climax.

"You're very responsive." He kissed her neck.

"How could I help it? You know just what to do." As soon as she recovered the power of speech, Emily asked him a question. "Can I return the favor and wash your hair?"

"And other parts of me?" He raised his eyebrows.

"We'll see," Emily said primly.

They both turned around in the bathtub, and soon Emily was washing his hair. After she finished the task, she followed his example and reaching around him gently, exploring his body with her soapy hands. She worked her way gently down his body until she finally grasped him in her soapy fingers. He stopped her, covering her hands with his. He was breathing heavily.

Chapter Fourteen

"You are so wonderful, Emily." He leaned back against her, savoring the feel of her wet body pressed up against his. "But we have to stop now because we're not going to make love in the tub."

"But we are already making love," she protested. "Just not having sex."

"You're right, of course, we are. Even this is probably a sin, but this is as far as we're going to go before we get married." He still held her hands firmly. "After that it's anything, and anywhere goes. The bathtub, kitchen counters, the barn, heck, maybe even in bed!"

"On horseback?" she wondered.

"I won't object if the horse doesn't." David laughed. "Emily, you amaze me. You're so innocent in so many ways, and in others you have a very wicked mind. Yes, we can make love on the horse."

"That sounds good to me, for later. But for now I may be naïve, David, but can't we go to bed and just cuddle. Please?"

"You know, I think we should get brownie points for resisting temptation." Emily winked at him. "Maybe sainthood."

"I don't think that's how it works." He laughed.

David couldn't resist any longer. It sounded like delicious torture but he was eager to sleep with Emily, as innocently as possible. Silently, he prayed for strength. They rinsed off and stepped out of the tub. They dried each other off and, wearing the terry cloth robes supplied by the hotel, turned their attention to drying each other's hair. David was standing behind Emily, brushing and blow drying her hair when his patience finally ended.

"Emily?" His voice was husky with emotion. "Don't you think your hair is dry enough?"

Emily nodded at David's image in the mirror, speechless. David stepped away from Emily and, his eyes meeting hers in the mirror, he untied the belt to his robe and let it drop to the floor. Then he went to a drawer and pulled some briefs and a T-shirt.

"You don't need to cover up now," Emily said softly, "I've seen it all."

"Trust me," David grinned ruefully, "I need to wear something to bed, and so do you."

He stepped back towards Emily and reached around her waist to unite her robe, letting it join his on the tile floor. She walked over and got a pair of shorts and a T-shirt and put them on. She turned to face him and he lifted her up, carrying her to the king-sized bed. He had turned down the covers before joining her in the tub, so all he had to do was gently lay her in the middle of the bed.

Emily lay on the bed, looking up at David with trust and love in her eyes. She reached one hand out to him. He joined her on the bed and took her in his arms, covering her face with soft gentle kisses that grew ever so slowly in warmth and passion. Emily met him kiss for kiss, her hands running gently over his neck and shoulders.

"I hate to say this but we'd better stop, these kisses are tempting. And also, you should call room service and feed me. One small bowl of strawberries does not constitute dinner for two, and I think," she grinned at him, a wide and wicked grin, "you're going to need something to eat to keep your strength up at the show tomorrow since we may have trouble getting any sleep tonight."

"Nagging already?" David grinned as he reached for the phone. "Good grief, woman. What do you want to eat?"

"I don't know, surprise me," she said softly. "I can't think right now."

"Real food or some sinful dessert?" he asked.

"Right now, I feel like something sinful," she decided, giving him a teasing pout. "Since it's the only sin I'm allowing myself tonight."

"Good point."

David spoke briefly into the phone before hanging it up and turning back to Emily. "They said it would be about half an hour before our food arrives."

It wasn't even a full half hour before the room service waiter arrived with colas and a pair of hot fudge sundaes. He tipped the waiter and brought the sundaes into the bedroom. They both sat cross-legged on the bed and ate the ice cream treats in companionable silence. Once they were done, David put the tray outside the door and they turned out the light.

Surprisingly, once they turned off the light and cuddled in each others' arms, they both slept very well. The next morning, both of them were drowsy when the wake-up call came at six a.m., but Emily was very relaxed and content. David kissed her until she was wide awake and smiled to himself as he noticed how slow she was moving as she was getting out of the bed. She did a lot of lifting and moving setting things up the day before. He got up and pulled on a pair of faded jeans.

"Why don't you grab a hot bath, honey?" he offered. "I've got to run down to the fairgrounds to feed the horses. I'll be back in about half an hour or so."

"Don't you want me to come along?" she asked.

"I'll be right back. Why don't you order breakfast for us so we can eat when I get back?" he suggested. "We'll have to leave for the show at about 7:30."

By the time David came back from feeding the horses, Emily had taken her bath and gotten dressed in her jeans and a T-shirt. Her hair was pulled back into a ponytail and tied with a ribbon to match her t-shirt. They sat down and ate breakfast before heading for the fairgrounds. When they got to the fairgrounds they worked side by side quickly to clean out the stalls, not Emily's favorite job, and groom the horses. She also fed and walked the puppy. Then they saddled both horses and rode them over to the practice arena.

Emily worked Raider carefully, getting him warmed up and loosened up for the show. She also concentrated on getting him to relax in the unfamiliar surroundings. David worked Target quietly on the rail, not making any special effort to practice turns with him or work him at any real speed. With Target all he needed to do was get his muscles warm and loose.

Emily expected David to get on Raider and take him through the poles that were up for practice but instead he watched as she took him through some practice runs. He made some quiet comments and suggestions, giving her lots of praise for how much she had learned since the first time he'd taken her riding.

Finally they took the horses back to the barn so that David could change into his good jeans and his Western shirt for the show. They tied up the horses and stepped into the tack room. David took a garment bag and unzipped it. He seemed almost hesitant as he turned to Emily.

"Emily?" He got her attention. "There's something I forgot to tell you about this show."

"What's up?" She was instantly curious, and from his tone she knew something was on his mind.

"I didn't enter myself on Raider," he said almost hesitantly.

"Then why did you bring him here?" she asked, faintly suspicious.

"I entered you on Raider in the novice class," he told her.

"David, I can't," she protested. "I barely know how to ride."

"Yes, you can. Think about it. Would I have entered you if I didn't think you were ready?" he prodded. "I don't care if you win or lose, just have fun, and try to give him a good smooth ride. You've been doing it at home, now go do it here. Okay?"

"I don't have any show clothes," she protested.

David handed her a second garment bag. "I hope you like the shirt, I had Nicole pick it out."

"Thank you, David." She kissed his cheek then looked at the shirt. "I hope it fits but I think the size is too small."

"Nicole said you'd say that. Try it on." David held out a ribbon and a western tie, both color coordinated to go with the shirt.

Emily put on the shirt and was surprised to realize that it fit perfectly. "How did she know?"

"It's her job," he reminded her. "Emily, she picked out some new jeans, too."

"That's very nice of her but I have jeans, and these are fairly new." Emily looked down at her jeans.

"They're way too large for you," David smiled at her, "and they used to be fairly tight."

"I knew I had lost some weight," Emily was pleased that he had noticed, "but not so much that I thought it would show."

"You've not only lost weight, you've firmed up your muscle tone. I've noticed for some time but I didn't want to pressure you or to make you feel that it was too important to me. I want to be happy for you and support you but you have to do what's best for yourself. You can't worry too much about how I feel about it because I love you whether you lose weight or not."

"That's how I've always found you David, very supportive while not filling me with pressure, it's part of why I love you." She hugged him before looking at the jeans. "Good grief! These are two sizes smaller than my other pair, they'll never fit."

But to her immense joy, they not only fit they were even a little bit loose.

Giving her a big wink, David handed her a tooled Western belt with a small buckle on it. "I would have gotten you a fancy buckle, but I thought you should go out and win one."

"Yeah, sure," she said drily, "I can hardly wait. I'm sure I'll win one sometime before the end of the century."

Emily threaded the belt through the loops on her jeans and they went out and got on the horses. Emily's slight jitters conveyed themselves to Raider, and she could feel the edge of tension in his massive body. She worked him slowly, trying to calm herself and the big gelding. When the first novice event was called, Keyhole race, right after the ponies, she was as ready as she would ever be.

"Now use your own judgment, Emily. You can work him easily through the event, and just use this show for practice, or you can go for it. Raider's been doing all right for you in Keyhole, but it's a tricky event." David grinned. "At least you'll be among the last to ride so you'll know what you have to do to win a ribbon."

Keyhole, an event that consisted of running a horse into a small chalk circle with an alley leading into the center, turning and running back through the finish line, was an event that could be plagued by disqualifications. Every time a horse stepped on or out of the chalk lines that horse and rider was disqualified. Sometimes the last rider in the class only had to stay in to place or even win the event.

This was not exactly the case for Emily though because several riders before her had good runs. She could go slow and careful to get a fourth place ribbon, or try to do a decent ride and hope to stay in and place even higher. Waiting was killing Emily, and this event traditionally ran slowly. Although the top times were under 10 seconds, after every rider, the judge and his crew had to look at the horses' tracks, rake the ground so it was smooth, and often repair the chalk circle.

Taking several deep breaths, Emily entered the arena. Following David's advice, she carefully lined the horse up with the alley to the keyhole. She picked the reins, clicked softly to the big horse and then they took off. Her ride was fast for a novice, although much slower than some of the more experienced riders that would follow. She focused her attention on stopping the horse at the correct moment and turning him back on his hindquarters to head for the finish line. When she finished the race she waited for what seemed like hours while the judge looked at the ground in and around the keyhole, carefully studying the tracks made by Raider, before he ruled it a "good ride."

David leaned over from on top of Target to give her a big kiss. "Good ride!" he congratulated her. "Do you know what place you're in?"

"No, but I know it's in the ribbons. I'm in shock." She smiled widely, exhilarated.

They watched the last novice rider run out and get disqualified, and then the next class of keyhole riders began, the twelve and under riders. Some shows had award ceremonies after every age group but the management at this show waited until all the keyhole age groups were complete.

Because the show was so large, Emily had time to tie up Raider. Then she got the puppy and went to sit in the stands and watch the event. David kept walking Target around, keeping him limber and loose until his class, the senior riders, had their turn. David ran beautifully, a good clean ride. Right after David's ride, Emily put the puppy back and got Raider out. She had barely mounted him before they were called in to receive their awards. David placed a very respectable second for his ride, but the shocker was Emily, she won her group! Her time wasn't spectacular but it held up against the other novices. She even heard one rider mutter as she received the trophy.

"I suppose she thinks she's fooling anyone, claiming to be a novice but I know better. Look at how good she did," the anonymous girl complained.

"That's not fair!" Emily protested to David. "You know I'm a real novice, for Pete's sake it was my first event ever!"

"Emily, relax and think about it, she paid you a huge

compliment." He pointed out, "She thinks you're too good to be a novice."

"Now that you mention it, it is a pretty strong compliment." Emily smiled. "Even if it was only sour grapes talking."

"Just think how she'd feel if she knew it was not only your first show, but also Raider's!" David laughed. "It would kill her."

"Now that I've tasted victory, I'm going to go all out the rest of the day." Emily suddenly felt competitive. "Her grapes are going to get very sour before this show is over."

David just laughed, pleased and surprised at the burst of competitive energy coming from Emily. This was a whole new woman!

The next few events went well for both Emily and David. She placed second in pole bending, fourth in birangle, and got another second in single pole. David was first in poles, second in birangle, and first in single poles. His real fun was watching Emily. With every ride she seemed to grow more confident. By the lunch break, she practically glowed with pride in Raider.

Chapter Fifteen

Emily wasn't entered in the next two events: flag race, and hurry scurry. David told her he hadn't entered her because they had never practiced those events and they were both pretty complex for a novice rider. In flag race, the rider had to exchange the flag in his hand for another one by sticking the flag into a bucket of sand on top of a barrel, and grabbing the one that was waiting there. He had to do this twice in the course. Most of the novices were disqualified.

Emily watched the action and said, "Hey! I could have gotten a ribbon in that event!"

"I know and I would have entered you in it but I don't like running flag race with a green horse." David explained, "The rider tends to stop the horse at the barrel and fool around with the flag, which I think confuses a horse that's learning to run around these barrels without slowing down."

"That makes sense." Emily nodded. "Why am I not in scurry?"

"Because in scurry there are jumps, small jumps, but jumps. Neither you nor Raider has ever been trained to jump, so I thought you might want to pass on that."

"Good thinking," she said with a grin.

David won the flag race and Emily was amazed at how he could exchange the flags without slowing his horse down. His hand-eye coordination was fantastic! He also did well in scurry, with Target racing over the jumps as if they weren't there. With one event to go for the day, he was leading his age group for the high point award. The shock was that in her class, Emily was in third place, but only one point behind second and three behind first.

The last event of the day was figure eight race, in which a rider had to turn either left or right at one end of the arena, and the opposite direction at the other. For this event the timing line was in the center of the arena.

The thing that made this event difficult for some horses was the second turn. That turn was at the same end of the arena as the gate they entered and left by. For these horses, this was the end of the arena where the finish line usually was and this was where they were going to stop, no matter what the darn rider wanted to do.

Fortunately, Raider avoided this bad habit. He seemed to listen as Emily steered him away from the direction of the gate and back to the finish line. She won the event and moved up into second place in the novice high point standings. Emily and David took care of the horses, walking them out and making sure they were cool and ready to be put away before feeding them and giving them grain and fresh water. They also fed and walked the puppy, who was very popular with the other riders.

"Do you want to go back to the hotel and get dressed up so we can go out to eat?" David asked, sitting on a chair outside the tack room. "Or we can go back to the hotel and just get room service. We can also clean up here and eat at the club barbecue, lady's choice."

"If we get to the hotel, I won't want to go out again." She decided, "I think I'd rather have barbecue here, but where do we get cleaned up?"

"They have showers in the restrooms in the barns. That's because when they have horse racing here, some of the exercise riders and grooms actually live in the barns."

"Then let's eat here before we get back to the hotel," she grinned, "and the bed."

"I've created a monster," David moaned dramatically.

"No, you've created a very tired but happy woman." She

laughed at him.

They each took quick, and unfortunately cold, showers in the fairground restrooms before changing into clean jeans and shirts. They walked over to the picnic area and each got a plate filled with the most wonderful barbecued beef, baked beans, coleslaw and corn on the cob. There was an assortment of cakes and pies for dessert, and plenty of hot black coffee, iced tea, soft drinks, and milk. Emily noticed, however, that many of the adults had brought beer.

At one point, when David went over to get more BBQ beef, Emily saw a man that looked slightly familiar. The man spotted David and went over to him.

"Hi David, I see you had some great rides today." She then heard him say, "By the way, who was that riding your colt?"

"Cliff, you met Emily before at our charity show. I've been teaching her to ride." He smiled to himself at Cliff's expression.

"That's Emily? But she was afraid of horses, and she looks different, too." By this time the men had walked back to Emily. "Howdy ma'am, I'm sure glad to see you again, even if I didn't recognize you."

"I was covered with dirt when we met, no wonder you didn't recognize me." Emily smiled at Cliff. "It's good to see you again."

"You've sure learned to ride really well." Cliff sipped his beer. "I can't believe it."

"Thanks," Emily beamed, "David has been a fantastic trainer."

"What you haven't heard, Cliff, is that Emily and I are going to be married soon," David surprised the older man.

"Congratulations! To both of you." Cliff was surprised and very pleased. "I must say David, you found a real gem here."

"Yes, I think so." David kissed Emily softly.

After the barbeque there was a live band playing country music. Emily and David sat by the fire and listened, but neither of them wanted to dance. It had been a long day and Emily was all too aware, in every muscle, that she had never ridden for such a long time before.

When they returned to the hotel room, they were both tired from the long day at the show and from having such a full meal. Emily was getting stiff. They took a long hot bath, turning on the water jets in the spa tub, before getting into bed and drifting off to sleep in each other's arms.

The next morning, Sunday, was a repeat of the day before with one exception. Once again Emily got showered, dressed, and ordered breakfast while David went to the barn and fed the horses. They ate breakfast together and then left for the show. There was a small, colorful, but meaningful worship service held in one of the barns before the show started. Not all the riders attended, but there was a good turnout.

"This is weird, great, but weird," Emily whispered

"Jesus was born in a stable," David whispered back.

"True, still. . ." She smiled. "Well, I guess it's better to have a service here than to ignore the Lord's Day."

Emily had a very good day at the show. She placed second in quadrangle, third in poles II, a variation of the pole bending course, and won the speed barrels and barrels. David won quad, poles II, and speed barrels but he placed second in barrels. At the end of the day both of them won their respective high point awards. Emily was on cloud nine, absolutely amazed, as she collected her prize--a large ornate silver belt buckle.

This day seemed slightly shorter to Emily. The routine was more familiar, and the courses Emily was entered in were the ones she had spent the most time practicing. At the end of the day, when she had put Raider away, she sat on a chair in the tack room relaxing with the very tired puppy sleeping in her lap. She knew she should begin packing her things, but she just seemed to drift in the chair, almost joining the puppy in sleep.

"Emily, I have an idea." David walked over and kissed her gently. "Let's call home and see if they're okay, and if they are, then let's pack up all the stuff we don't need tonight and stay overnight. We can head for home early tomorrow."

"That makes sense. If we stay we can have a nice evening but if we leave tonight, we have to load all this stuff you brought and the horses, and then hit the road."

"Not only that, but if it took us two hours to eat and get everything ready to go, we'd arrive home at about one a.m.," he pointed out.

"And still have to put the horses away," she moaned.

"And, we wouldn't get to sleep together," he added.

"I'll call home." Emily dug up her cell phone. When she returned, her face was shining. "Julia said for us to stay and have fun. She said things are under control. I told her we'd be home tomorrow sometime around noon."

"Great, let's go have dinner." David was relieved.

"Can we take a bath first?" she pleaded.

"Of course," he said, then suggested, "together?"

"Naturally." She sat the puppy down and stood up, smiling. He hugged her.

"And cuddle in bed after dinner?" She snuggled against him.

"All night," he promised.

"Gee," she said with exaggerated innocence, "I had wondered why we didn't check out of our room this morning. I sure hope you'll be able to stay awake for the drive home tomorrow."

"We'll worry about that in the morning. But for now," he pulled her into his arms, "we have a date with a bathtub."

They went back to the hotel. In short order they were both in the bathtub, soaping and teasing each other into a frenzy like they had on the first night.

"We should stop if we're going out for dinner."

"Can't we eat here?" Emily asked. "Dinner in bed?"

She kissed his neck.

"Stop that!" He gently swatted her behind. "We're going out! One of my favorite restaurants is here in this town and I'd like to share it with you."

"Okay. I'll get dressed." She went to the closet and pulled out a new dress. It was off the shoulders and brightly colored with a swirling skirt, a real change from the kind of dresses she wore in the past.

"Emily, you look spectacular!" David looked pretty good himself. He had dressed in nice crisp slacks and a tailored shirt. "Let's go eat."

"And then let's come back here, I think we need to spend a long night in bed," she suggested.

"We need the rest," he agreed.

"We do need the rest," she grinned at him wickedly, "and we'll have a good night."

They went to David's favorite restaurant, a steakhouse that served the best steaks Emily had ever eaten, along with large salads with tangy dressing, huge baked potatoes, and some excellent, crusty sourdough bread. Every time they needed anything a waiter appeared instantly, and yet they never had the impression that he was hovering over them. The atmosphere was relaxed, with people dressed in everything from western wear to fancy dress suits and lovely gowns. In the background there was a country western band playing lively but not raucous music.

"Would you care for dessert?" David asked. "They have a fantastic dessert tray."

"This is a great restaurant, David," Emily told him. "I don't know when I've ever had such good food, and the service has been impeccable. I'd probably love anything on the dessert tray, but I couldn't eat another bite."

"Let's go for a walk before we head back to the hotel," he suggested.

"Good idea." Hand in hand, they left the restaurant.

By the time they made it back to the hotel they were more than ready to settle in the bed and talk before they drifted off to sleep. They awoke in each other's arm, shared a leisurely shower, checked out of the hotel and left for the show grounds.

David fed the horses and pulled the trailer around. While the horses ate, they both loaded the rest of their show equipment into the trailer. It was amazing how quickly they dismantled the tack room, leaving it bare. David put hay and grain into the trailer for the horses to eat on the way home. Then he led Raider out, blanketing him, and putting his leather hood on his head before turning his attention to bandaging his legs. Emily took down the buckets and hooks in Raider's stall, and raked the soiled straw out in front of the barn. She started to do the same in Target's stall, but the older horse wanted to cuddle with her. He followed her over to his empty grain bucket and put his long nose into it, searching for traces of food.

"Get back, brat." She slapped the big horse affectionately. Finally she gave up and haltered him, leading him out and tying him to a hitching post. Then she finished cleaning out his stall. David finished with Raider, and Emily walked him around while David then bandaged Target and loaded him. Finally she led the big colt up to the trailer and slapped his broad butt to get him to walk in. Quickly he shut the door behind him, and put the padded chain up behind his tail. David reached into a front door of the trailer and fastened his rope. Then he checked the trailer hitch and the lights before they got in and started the long drive home. They stopped for a snack at a fast food place around ten, and arrived at David's ranch shortly after noon. Nicole was there and she helped as they unloaded the horses and put them away.

Nicole took David aside and said, "We decided not to say anything when Emily called last night, but I think she should go home and check on her father right away. He didn't want her to come home early, but even I can tell he's worse."

"Thanks, Sis." David kissed her cheek and looked over at Emily with sadness and tenderness in his eyes. "I'll take care of things. Will you finish with the horses?"

"Sure. Hey, tell Emily I'm proud of her for doing so well."

Nicole walked over to the barn.

"Emily, Nicole is going to finish the horses. I'm going to take you home." He took a deep breath and said, "Your father isn't doing very well and he didn't want us to know until we got home."

"I was worried when he didn't come on the line last night. I've been dreading this for so long. Is he hospitalized?" Emily tried to be brave.

"No, but remember, Emily, he has a doctor's appointment today at two, so we'll have to see what happens then." David hugged her gently. "Let me go in and call my secretary so my appointments can be rescheduled."

"Did you have any scheduled for today?" she asked.

"Just one for later tonight." David looked at her gently. "And I may not be able to reschedule this one, but I'll try."

"Thank you David, I really need you now." Emily leaned into his warmth for a moment before they got into his car and he drove her home.

Chapter Sixteen

The short drive to Emily's house seemed endless, and still in a strange way, far too short. After David parked in front of her house, he turned to Emily. He hugged her gently, noting her pale skin and the traces of tears in her eyes.

"I want to stay with you, Emily, but I have to leave for a while." He kissed her forehead. "I'll be back as soon as I can."

"I know." She smiled softly. "I'll be all right."

She watched him for a moment as he drove away down her narrow street before turning to go into the house. As she reached for the door, Julia opened it.

"Your father's in the den in front of the TV. He's as comfortable as possible, but he's not doing well at all." She hugged Emily with compassion and sadness in her eyes. "I wanted to call you but he insisted that we let you have your weekend."

Emily nodded silently and went in search of her father, bracing herself not to react to his condition. She wished David could be with her but she knew he had some things to take care of.

David parked his car and went to help Nicole with the horses. Together they took off the leg wraps and blankets, and put both horses on the hot walker for a moment to make sure they were walking normally. They put new bedding in their stalls, tossed a flake of hay in each of their mangers, and measured out grain for each of them. David checked the automatic waterers in each stall. Finally, he unhitched each horse from the walker and stabled them. Then he parked the trailer in it's usual space, unhooked it and parked the truck. He went into the house and quickly made some calls before he drove his car back to join Emily. He needed to be there, for Pete of course, but even more for Emily.

Emily could see the decline in her father's health at first glance, his skin was pale and clammy, and his breathing was slow and labored. She knew her father well enough to keep her emotions in check. As weak as he was, she could still see his fighting spirit and yet both of them knew the fight was near its end.

"Daddy! I would have come home if you'd called." She hugged him gently and kissed his cheek.

"That's why I didn't call," he said, his tone weak and thready. "I told Julia not to let you know."

"Why, Daddy?" she asked, a hint of tears in her eyes.

"Because it wouldn't make a bit of difference and you know it." He coughed a little then said, "And it was the first time you've had anything for yourself in so long. Was it wonderful?"

"Yes, Daddy." She smiled, struggling to hold back the tears. "I had the most wonderful weekend ever."

"And was it romantic, being with David?" He managed to smile at her.

"Daddy, it was more than romantic." Emily smiled softly. "David's a fantastic man, and he cares so much for me. I can barely understand it, but that's how it is."

"All that means is he's smart," he managed. "And how was the horse show? Did David win a lot of trophies?"

"Yes, Daddy, he always does." She smiled softly then added, "And the horse show was great. David had a big surprise for me. He had me entered on Raider in the novice division and I won some trophies myself, and a belt buckle."

She held out the engraved silver buckle for him to see.

"Fantastic, Sweetie. I'm so proud of you. I always have been." He seemed to weaken in front of her eyes. "Now, let me rest until I have to see the doctor."

She kissed his forehead and tucked the quilt around him

before she left him to his nap.

As she left the room, she heard him barely whisper, "Emily, please, no hospital. Let me stay here."

The phrase "until I die" went unspoken, but she heard it clearly.

She went up to her room for a while and sat on the edge of her bed. She had her moment to let go and cry. Then she rinsed her face and went down to find David had returned. He was in the kitchen with her mother. As usual, Mae seemed to be unaware of what was happening, but she knew something was terribly wrong. She had tears in her eyes. David was holding her hand and talking to her gently.

Julia drew the older woman away so David could be alone with Emily. "How is he?"

"He hasn't got long. It's so clear that I know it even without the doctor. The worst thing for me is that he's aware of what's happening. I was hoping that when he got to this stage he wouldn't be, but he is. He doesn't want to go into the hospital and I know the doctor's going to want to admit him. I'm dreading this appointment."

"I'll be with you, if that helps." David drew her even closer, letting her cry and giving her what comfort he could. In the short time he'd known Pete, he'd come to really like and admire Emily's father.

It wasn't long, only about half an hour, before David drove Pete and Emily to the medical center where Pete's doctor had an office. The doctor had been alerted by Julia and had tried to clear his schedule so that there were very few patients in the waiting room. Pete's deterioration was clear to every member of the office staff, and they all took time to give both Pete and Emily a hug and a kind word.

That didn't stop the receptionist from winking and grinning at the office manager out of sight of Emily before saying, "Hey Linda, looks like Emily found a hot one. Wow! Good for her."

"And the timing's perfect," the manager shot back, "because he seems even nicer than he looks." She sighed softly. "I hope he is that nice because she'll need him. And soon."

"I know, I've prayed for her and Pete," she looked at Linda, "and Mae too, of course. I wonder how she met him, do you know?"

"Kate and Laura, of course." Linda looked at the single and very pretty receptionist and asked, "Have you met either of them? No, don't bother to answer, I know you haven't."

"Why?"

"It's easy," Linda smiled, "you're still single."

In the exam room the doctor's appointment proved to be every bit as difficult as Emily feared. Pete's doctor wanted to admit him to the hospital straight from the office. He was ready to call an ambulance to transport him. Pete, as expected, balked.

"They can't do anything for me, so why should I go into the hospital?" he argued, his voice was weak but his attitude was strong. "Can't I stay home with my family?"

Emily took the doctor aside. "Exactly why should he go into the hospital, Doctor?"

"He's dying," the doctor said gently. "Surely you've realized that by now."

"Will being in a hospital save him?" she returned.

"No, but we may be able to prolong his life," the doctor admitted.

"By making him less comfortable, putting him in unfamiliar surroundings, putting tubes in him, and having him cared for by strangers? No, thank you. We'll take him home." Emily told the doctor firmly, "I have a Registered Nurse living with me, so between the two of us we'll make him as comfortable and happy as we can, but we'll do it at home."

David stepped behind Emily, his arms around her waist, giving her his strength. She took a deep breath then said, "Doctor, if he was unaware of his surroundings I'd probably go along with your plans, but he's alert and he should make his own choices. We're taking him home."

"Refill his pain prescriptions and make him comfortable," the doctor relented, "and call me if you need me. Don't tell anyone, but for Pete, I'll make a house call."

"Thank you, Doctor," Emily said quietly.

He touched her face gently and said, "Pete's lucky to have you for his daughter."

They took Pete home. David helped the older man as he walked up the steps and into the house. They settled him in his favorite chair and sat with him until he fell asleep in front of the TV. Then Emily and David sat in the kitchen and talked to Mae, who for once seemed to be aware of her surroundings.

"I'm so sorry, Emie, that your father and I are such a burden on you," she told Emily. "I'm so proud of you for how well you take care of us."

"I love you, Mom. What else can I do?" Emily smiled sadly at her mother.

"Your new friend is so handsome, Emily," Mae told her daughter. "I hope he makes you happy."

"He does, Mom." Emily sighed.

"I'd love to see you married and happy." She continued, "I just hope when it happens, I can remember who you are. I want you to realize, Dear, that even when I don't seem to be able to think straight, I do know that I love you."

"I know you do, I love you too, Mom," Emily told her.

As suddenly as her rationality had come, it fled. Abruptly, Mae got off her chair and crawled under the table. "Really, sis, you should get down here and take care of this baby. You shouldn't just let him crawl over by the stove like that."

"Sorry Mom," Emily apologized ironically, "I didn't see him. I thought he was still in his playpen." She pretended to pick something up off the floor, and keeping her back to Mae, left the room briefly.

"Is that your baby?" Mae looked at David. "Are you my sister's husband?"

"Yes, Mae," he answered her, "my name is David, remember?"

"No, but I don't seem to have a very good memory," Mae admitted. "Can I ask you something? Who's that sick man in the living room?"

"He's your husband, Pete," David told her gently.

"He must be very ill," Mae said sadly. "He looks so old I hardly recognize him."

"Yes, Mae. He is very ill," David told her, "that's why Emily and I are here."

David took Emily aside and hugged her gently before saying, "Emily, I have all the arrangements ready, we can get married tonight if you'd like, at my place. I took a chance and made a few calls today. That way, Pete can be there. I even managed to invite his doctor."

"Yes, we should do it tonight." She had tears in her eyes. "I want to have my father there when I get married. I don't care about the rest. The flowers, the cake, fancy food or even a lot of guests. I just need him there. So I do want us to get married tonight. I want you beside me day and night, good times and bad."

"Well gee, I guess I will." David pretended to sulk. "You could at least say you love me when you demand we get married."

"I thought the bit about wanting you beside me day and night in good times and bad was a pretty good declaration of love!" She pouted.

"Well, the words would make it perfect," David said stiffly.

"The words?" Emily smiled then said, "You mean the words: I love you?"

"Well, yeah, those words," David said softly. "Do you love me as much as I love you?"

"What would you do if I said I love you more? You opened

142

me up to the wonder of life, and the joy of love. How could I resist? I do love you, so much that it's hard to put into words. I do know one thing: the future doesn't scare me anymore. I'd even like to have your children, one day"

An unbelievable joy filled David. "Well, in that case, I guess I will marry you today. I've already made calls to everyone to help us set it up." David kissed her. "Isn't it lucky that Nikki's in town now?"

"Very lucky." She smiled, tears in her eyes. "But don't you have to work today?"

"I did have a couple of appointments set up for today but I had my secretary cancel all but one and clear my schedule for a few days," David kissed her, "so I only have to go in for that one. It should only take half an hour."

"While you're doing that, I can pack a few things, fun a few errands, and . . ." Her voice trailed off.

"What is it?" David asked gently. "Do you need more time? Please say no."

"It's not that. It just hit me, why we're getting married so soon. Emily shook a little, trying to fight off her sorrow and concentrate on the joy of marrying the man she loved.

"We'll tell everyone to meet at the ranch at. . . what do you think? Around seven?" At Emily's dazed nod he continued, "We'll have a limo pick us up at your house." David got up and began dressing as he planned. "Your folks and Julia can take it home after the ceremony."

"Okay, I better hit the road if I'm going to make it on time." Emily's smile was so wide it seemed to be a permanent addition to her face, but it didn't quite reach her eyes. "I have a lot to do."

They kissed and separated to go their separate ways, each with a long mental list of errands to get done. They each had a million thoughts bouncing around in their heads.

Emily took her car and headed out to run her errands. She called Nikki and told her what was going on, but Nick already knew. After she and Nick exchanged a short and excited conversation, Emily got to the point of her call.

"I want to wear that wedding dress I modeled a few weeks ago," she told Nikki. "Remember you had them alter it for me instead of just pinning it temporarily? It was so perfect for me. Do you think we can get it?"

"Why do you think I told them to alter it to fit you?" Nikki smiled through the phone. "It's all ready for you at Hans' studio. I bought it for you, just in case. I'll call him to let him know you'll be picking it up."

"You're terrific, Nick." Emily gushed. "Do me one more favor? Don't tell David I called you; let me surprise him with the dress."

"I will, and Emily?" She paused. "I'm gonna be the best sister-in-law you ever had."

"You're gonna be the only sister-in-law I'll ever have, and I couldn't have chosen anyone I loved more."

She finally arrived home with her dress in a garment bag. Emily began packing a few things to take over to David's: her make-up, dress, shoes, veil, and a few more things. She sat down with Mae and told her about the wedding. She got Mae cleaned up and dressed, ready to go. She made sure Mae was dressed in her best outfit. She told Pete to put on his best suit, and Julia helped her with him. He was tired, but excited. Emily put her garment bag by the door along with anything else she was taking so they'd be ready for David.

David quickly finished his own errands. He had already called Nick and took the mandatory teasing a sister is required to give her brother when he tells her he's getting married. He had called as many members of both Churches as he knew and explained the situation before the weekend, adding that he couldn't be sure when the wedding would take place. Most of the women had made casseroles and had them waiting in the freezer, ready for when they were needed. So he knew they had plenty of food. It would be potluck but plentiful, and among the Church members were two caterers. Both of them also had some of their best dishes ready to go.

Also among the Church ladies was a woman named Grace who baked spectacular wedding cakes. She had a four-tiered cake in her cooler, covered with very realistic edible flowers. Everyone who knew Pete loved him, and the ones who didn't know Pete knew David and knew he was always ready to help someone out.

He made calls from his house and made arrangements for several things. He had his cleaning service out to give the house a fast, but detailed cleaning from top to bottom. He had a florist lined up to do silk floral arrangements in the great room downstairs. He called his friends and family, and also called Emily's. He made sure there was lots of champagne and strawberries, and sparkling cider for Mae. The four-tiered wedding cake arrived. The topper was a cowboy and cowgirl sitting on horseback. It was just the light touch of humor the cake needed. Grace had done a beautiful job with it. He already had the ring, ready and waiting. He called for a limo to drive him over to Emily's.

He got out of the limo and walked up to the front door. He raised his hand to knock, but Emily managed to sneak up behind him. He turned and looked at her, awed and amazed at the love that spread through him. Life was good. His quick laugh was filled with joy.

"Hurry up gorgeous, we have a wedding to get to. Ours!"

Chapter Seventeen

In spite of the rush to put the wedding on and the sorrow behind the reason for the rush, it was a beautiful and touching wedding. The pastors from both Emily's and David's churches took part in the ceremony. The flowers were beautiful, but silk instead of real flowers, in a nod to Pete's allergies. Of course, David's dogs were banished from the house and it had been meticulously cleaned, top to bottom, including the carpets. It was a last minute job, but a large tip to his cleaning service did wonders.

Emily dressed in Nicki's bedroom, putting on the beautiful designer gown she'd once modeled. It was ivory with a beaded halter top, mermaid silhouette, and a short, lacy train. Hans sent his favorite stylist over to do her hair and make-up. She looked amazing. While she was dressing, her father knocked on the door and came in.

"Honey, you look wonderful. I'm so proud of you, and so happy to see this day arrive," he said with misty eyes. "David's a wonderful man. He's everything I'd hoped you'd find. God has truly blessed us with him."

"Daddy, I couldn't settle for less, I had you." Emily fought back tears of her own. "I love you so much."

"Emily," her father started, "don't be sad, sweetie. God gave us a miracle to let me be here today. Always remember how proud I am of you and how much I love you. Whatever happens I will always be with you, in your heart, your memories, and your soul. We have that, and we have today. It's enough."

"I know," Emily swallowed hard, "and I am grateful, but Daddy. . ."

He hugged her and said, "Thank God for what he's given you and try not to worry about what you don't have, okay?"

Emily nodded wordlessly.

Emily's mother looked wonderful. Mae was dressed in a soft blue gown, lightly beaded, and her hair was perfectly styled. She was smiling and upbeat, although no one could tell if she realized what was going on.

Pete was in a dark grey suit. It had been perfectly tailored, but was now loose and his frailty was apparent, as was his joy. With his suit he wore a crisp white shirt and a slate blue tie. David's mother flew in for the special occasion. She was youthful in spite of her age, and beautiful in peach silk. Nicole was as gorgeous as always in a stylish burgundy gown. She acted as the maid of honor. David's law partner was the best man. The law partner couldn't believe his luck at standing next to a genuine supermodel. His smile almost split his face open.

For the other guests there were the members of both Churches, staff from David's office, a few members of the riding club and the matchmaking friends Kate and Laura, with their husbands and kids in tow. For what started out to be a small, last minute wedding, it was surprisingly large.

Pete was in a wheelchair most of the time but he found the strength to walk Emily up to where the pastors and David were waiting. No one could tell that Emily was supporting her father on that walk.

The ceremony itself was short and simple, touching and beautiful. One of the pastors said that Emily and David were proof of God's love and that miracles still happen.

David told Emily that while some people may think she was lucky to find him, he was the lucky one because Emily was simply everything to him, friend and lover and soul mate. Emily told David that he was the answer to questions she never thought to ask, and that she believed God had sent him to her.

After the ceremony they had a buffet with all the food

prepared by the ladies from both Churches. Almost everything a person could want to eat was there. Emily herself had little appetite but she appreciated how so many of her friends had contributed to the feast. It was more than joy in her day, it was a tribute to what they all thought of Pete. David and Emily cut the wedding cake, and the door to the patio was opened for people to have more room.

David and Emily had a strange wedding night. They saw how weak Pete got during the ceremony, so they decided to stay at Emily's house with her parents. Kate and her husband volunteered to go fetch the dogs and stay at David's house to take care of them and the horses. The fact that they had three kids, with one on the way, and he had horses and a pool had almost nothing to do with it. Of course, Kate brought her own dogs, the Boston's were the parents of David's Boston.

David and Emily were both too worried to make love that first night, they just slept together and held each other for comfort. For the next few days, David stayed close to Emily, working from her house as much as possible. He was so caring, always supporting and comforting her. He dealt with Mae gently, and with limitless patience. Watching them together, Emily fell even more in love with him. He left for work when he couldn't reschedule, but he came back as soon as possible. His paralegals and secretary were in and out of Emily's house frequently, and they were also considerate and helpful.

Laura and Jack and Kate and Bob came over, bringing food and comfort. They helped with housework and sat and talked with Emily and her parents. Laura was amazed that Emily had gone off to the horse show for a weekend with David.

"I may win best matchmaker of the year for this one!" she quipped.

"It's true I fell in love after the horse show. I can't resist that copper-penny hair and those brown eyes," Emily raved, a gleam in her eyes.

"What?" Laura sat up straighter.

"Oh! You mean David." Emily managed a grin. "And here I was talking about Raider."

"But how about David?" Laura asked.

"Well, I love him, too," Emily said, "but he's not a horse."

"I'll bet he's a stud though." Laura laughed.

"The only thing is, you don't get the credit for this match." Emily grinned.

"What! Even if you give credit to Kate, she's my unofficial partner," Laura shot back. "I'd still get credit."

"Nope." Emily's grin grew wider. "This was a match made in Heaven and the credit goes to Him."

"Good Lord."

"Exactly." Emily was smug.

"But back to my . . .Oh oh," she said as her cell phone rang. Laura answered the call then she got up. "I'm sorry, I have to leave, my sitter wants me to get home."

Finally, a few days after the wedding, David knew it was the right time for them to make love. He made up a tray with crackers, cheese, and strawberries, then put a bottle of champagne on ice. He wanted to make sure they came together with all the tenderness and passion Emily had ever dreamed of.

Emily was an emotional mess, happy and depressed at the same time. Romance was the last thing on her mind. She was sure she had never felt less romantic in her life, and yet. . . She was impatient to be with David.

Dave sensed her mood, her pain and her nerves. He wanted everything to be perfect for her, and he wanted her. But still, he was a gentle man, "If you'd rather. . ."

"No, I want to." She smiled sadly. "I want to be with you."

David stood by the bed with a lazy grin on his face for a moment then slowly removed his watch. Holding her gaze, he pulled off his t-shirt and unsnapped his jeans. Her eyes went wide as he reached for the zipper but she was silent, watching him with love and trust in her eyes as he pulled his jeans off over his bare feet. His eyes locked with hers as he removed his briefs.

He gently undressed her, and they sat on the bed facing each other while feeding one another bites of cheese, crackers, and veggies from a tray he'd prepared. They also sipped champagne and savored some plump strawberries.

They kissed and sipped and nibbled and sipped and kissed some more. She nibbled on his neck and trailed her tongue along his collarbone. Her hands moved gently over his body, moved beyond words he let her have her gentle way with him. He was so close to exploding that it didn't last long. Champagne and food were forgotten, and loving exploration and tasting began.

He lowered his mouth to capture one breast, using his tongue and teeth to tease the nipple before turning his attention to the other breast. His hands roamed her body, gently exploring. Soon one hand slowly made its way lower and lower, his long fingers gently parting the folds of her moist feminine parts.

"David, please. Make love to me now," Emily pleaded.

He kissed her gently on her soft abdomen before raising his head and looking at her for a timeless moment. He slid his hands down her back and playfully squeezed her bottom. One finger slid along the valley between her cheeks exploring her gently, before he teased her by gently sliding his finger in and out and then teasing her bud. She reached between them and, for the first time slid her hand along his erection. It was very firm and large, more than ready for her.

In spite of her virginity the entrance was easy and relatively painless. She totally forgot her inhibitions and inner shyness. David held himself in check for a long moment.

"I love you Emily," he whispered against her hair as he began to thrust slowly and gently in a rhythm as old as time. Gradually the intensity built, both in the force of his thrusts and in their speed. Emily matched his rhythm perfectly, thrust for thrust. Unconsciously her heels locked around him at the base of his spine.

She practically burst into flames. As if he wasn't excited and aroused enough already Dave reacted to her exploding passion with his own. He was frenzied by the realization that he was the first man to awaken her. The rush of love he felt rocked him like he'd never felt before.

She began to make small sounds in the back of her throat as she felt herself nearing the brink. Soon, together they went over the precipice, whirling off into a place that, no matter how many couples had been there since time began, was theirs alone. Breathless, they held each other and drifted back to earth, savoring the sensation they shared in a silent communication. Emily smiled, content, and David kissed her gently. Together they lay there together, sated and temporarily drained.

"Are you all right?" he asked with tender concern.

"I'm perfect," she told him. "You're perfect."

"Won't you be too sore tomorrow?" he asked with concern.

"Who cares?" Emily smiled, reaching for him.

Chapter Eighteen

In the days that followed, all of Emily's friends came over to offer their support and prayers. In spite of that, and a new husband, Emily was filled with a deep sorrow, almost as if she was already grieving. Both of the preachers who'd officiated at her wedding offered spiritual comfort, prayers, and Bible readings, and some just plain hand holding. The preachers' families and members of both congregations came for quick visits. Some of the women helped with meals and household chores.

"I know how hard this is for you, Emily," her preacher said gently, "but it's a part of life. Don't let it defeat you. You must hold onto your faith. You have had a fantastic father, and now you have a wonderful husband and soon, God willing, you will have beautiful children."

"I know, Reverend Steinz, and I know God is good." She forced a smile. "He gave me David at just the right time, and I have some wonderful friends, more than I realized."

She looked at him and asked shyly, "Does it make me a horrible person to almost wish it was over?"

"No my dear. It makes you very human. For you, the hardest part is seeing your father in such pain. To watch him struggle when you know he's going to a better place. You'll miss him and grieve for him but you will also know he's in Heaven and not in pain any more."

Kate and Laura brought their husbands and kids. The men flirted with Emily's mother, which cheered her up. Even in her declining mental state, she knew something was terribly wrong. She was by turns confused, sad, and agitated. Still, she always perked up when she had handsome men flirting with her.

Nicole came over a few times, sometimes she came with David's law partner, and once she even brought Hans. They talked to Pete when he was awake, and to Mae when he wasn't. They also kept Emily company. Julia used her skills as a nurse to give Pete his medications and keep him as comfortable as possible, and gave Emily time to share quiet conversations with her father without having to act as his nurse.

"I really feel better knowing that you have David now. He's a very good man, Emily," Pete told his daughter on Friday afternoon.

"I know he's a good man, Daddy. I'm glad you like him." Emily kissed her father's hand firmly grasped in her own.

"Do you love him?" he asked.

"Very much, Daddy," she told him, her eyes shining.

"That's all I ask." Pete drifted off to sleep.

Later that afternoon Pete's breathing became even more strained, and he seemed to drift in and out of consciousness. Julia checked on him every few minutes, but for the most part she left him in Emily's hands. David came over to stand by Emily. They moved Pete from his position on the living room sofa into his bedroom.

Emily and David stayed by his side. Her pastor came over to pray with her, but left soon after that because he got a call from another parishioner who's son was terribly wounded in a traffic accident.

"I can stay here if you need me," he told Emily. "I can send an associate to the hospital."

"No thanks, Reverend," Emily told him with quiet dignity. "We know what's going to happen here and we've had time to get used to the idea, but Mrs. Walters must be frantic. She needs you more than I do. Tell her she has my prayers."

"God bless you Emily," He hugged her briefly, whispering a prayer. "I will tell her."

Shortly after midnight, Pete died.

Emily called Pete's doctor and told him. She knew what she had to do and what Pete's wishes were so she had things to keep her busy all day. In a strange way, making the funeral arrangements was a comfort to Emily because it gave her one last thing she could do for her father. Sitting at home would have been unbearable. Although David offered to help, and even volunteered the use of his secretary, she took care of things herself. She needed his warm hugs, his prayers, and his love, but she wanted to do as much as she could herself.

For Emily the hardest part was calling Pete's friends and the rest of the family. Emily called her relatives and the friends she knew fairly well. Some of them were cautious when it was her on the phone, knowing that it was probably bad news. The worst for Emily were the calls to people who were excited and happy to hear from her, until she told them why she was calling, and their happiness turned to grief. All of them felt the loss of a good man. Some of Pete's friends offered to help make the calls, but Emily wanted to do it herself. She leaned back into David's arms and kept dialing, going through Pete's address book.

She asked everyone not to come over until the next day, but soon friends of Mae and Pete came over, most bearing casseroles or baked goods and flowers. They offered tearful hugs and comfort food, but most importantly, they offered her love and let her know how much Pete meant to them. A local florist delivered several plants and floral arrangements. Mae stayed close to Emily all day. She seemed a little confused, slightly dazed, and very sad.

The day of the funeral was so beautiful, so bright and clear that Emily wished she could share it with her father. With a sigh, she dressed sedately, but not in black. She wore a soft powder blue dress with white trim and a wide white collar. It was a dress that highlighted her recent weight loss and fit her beautifully. It was also one of the dresses Pete told her she looked wonderful in. She clung to David for emotional support and still managed to look after her mother with a deceptively effortless calm.

Her serene outward demeanor was behind the only unexpected disturbance of the day. Although she was grieving, she had come to terms with the loss of her father. It had been harder to see him deteriorate than to actually lose him. Somehow she knew he was still with her. She could feel him there, but healthy and whole. She prayed his pain was gone forever and clung to her faith that he was in a better place. The simple graveside service was an ending, a farewell, but she never believed it was the last time she would feel her father's presence or his love. She never realized that her placid expression and dry eyes offended some of her relatives.

"She sure doesn't seem to be grieving, not at all," Emily overheard her aunt say to her cousin shortly after they arrived back at Emily's house. "All she seems to want to do is get this over with and mess around with that fancy new husband of hers."

"She didn't even wear black," her cousin replied, with a nasty tone, "and she looks better than I've ever seen her, with her hair and make-up done. It doesn't seem right to me."

"I'm glad you think Emily looks great," Nicole interrupted the two women. "I've been working with her on her hair and make-up. I've even got her some modeling work. Maybe you've heard of me, I'm Nikki Silver? And by the way, Pete loved her in that dress and he really loved to see her looking so good. He was really proud of her." Nicole moved away gracefully but she was furious at the two women.

As they intended, Emily heard the two women and she walked over to join them.

"Are you implying that there's something improper about having my husband at my father's funeral?" Emily jumped to her own defense, still speaking with that quiet dignity. "David and my father became very close in very short order. He couldn't have done anything more for my father or for me during a very hard time. In fact, he was by my side when I lost my father. On the other hand, how long has it been since you came to visit? Don't get me wrong, I love you and I love having you here. I respect your grief. I just would have preferred for you to come visit my father when was alive and he could still enjoy it, and I want you to respect my feelings too."

Behind her, David turned to Nicki and spoke quietly. "I've never understood why some people would make such judgmental, catty remarks at funerals. It seems like they think Emily is the only one who should show any respect for Pete."

He knew he'd been overheard when he heard gasps from the two women, so he walked over and took Emily's arm and led her away.

"Thanks." Emily smiled softly at him.

"I didn't have to tell them off, you had already said everything that needed saying. I did it because I wanted to," he told her softly.

"No. I meant thanks for being my husband," Emily whispered.

"Don't thank me, thank our matchmaker, and this time I won't give the credit to Kate and Laura. This time I think our matchmaker was a Higher Authority," David told her. "Is that such an outrageous idea?"

"No," Emily whispered back. "It seems the right answer and I thank Him for you every day."

Leaning over his shoulder to see who was watching, he kissed her gently on the cheek. "I love you, sweet Emily."

Chapter Nineteen

The first few weeks after her father's death were very difficult for Emily. She was an emotional stew. She had to deal with the grief and deep sense of loss from losing her father. She also had the joy that came from being newly married to a man she truly loved, a man who gave her unconditional support and who was a steady comfort to her. Her friends were also a source of comfort. Even with all that comfort and support it was still a constant struggle trying to cope with her emotions while also trying to handle her mother's deteriorating mental condition.

Her mother must have missed her husband on some level because she sank deeper into her senile dementia without Pete around. Some days she would be relaxed and calm, almost cheerful, even if she was not quite on the same wavelength as the rest of the world. Those days she was almost a joy to be around, looking at the world through childlike, innocent eyes.

Other days, she could also seem childlike but these days she resembled a spoiled child. She would be demanding and petulant, wearing Emily down. She wanted this, demanded that. The food wasn't to her liking. Her favorite show wasn't on TV. It was either too cold or too hot. Emily tried to fix Mae's favorite meals, to explain that the TV show she wanted to see had been cancelled ten years ago, tried to explain that she couldn't control the weather.

It was a strain on Emily at one of the hardest times in her life. Sometimes her patience would wear thin and she'd snap at Mae. Once she even lost her control completely and really yelled at her. Emily felt so bad about it that she had Julia watch Mae for a while, then went into her room and cried. Julia comforted her, telling her that even though she loved her mother, dealing with her dementia could try the patience of a saint, and reminding her that Mae would forget all about Emily yelling at her. She told Emily she should take a day off and go somewhere to relax, shop or see a movie, even grab a nice meal. Emily never crossed the line into physical abuse, and after that incident she never yelled at Mae again, but still, she felt guilty.

Then there were times Mae realized Pete was gone and mourned him deeply, sitting quietly in the living room staring at his empty chair, tears in her eyes. It was hard to comfort Mae at those times, but they passed relatively quickly.

Finally there were the days when Mae was not only petulant but also filled with paranoia. On those days, she would protest anything Julia or Emily tried to do for her. She would scream that she was being murdered during her bath, and beaten when one of them tried to remove her shoes and socks.

At one point a social worker, called by a neighbor who'd heard the screaming, came knocking on the door to investigate charges of senior abuse. Mae was thankfully having a good day when the social worker came around.

The hardest days for Emily, though, were thankfully rare. These were the days when she still thought she was twenty-five. She kept begging Emily to take her to see her parents. In reality, they were long since dead. On these days, her 'youth days' as Emily called them, the town seemed unfamiliar and changed. Nothing was the way she remembered it.

It could be funny too, and Emily learned you had to either laugh or cry. It was on one of those days that Emily took Mae to Disneyland, where they had annual passes. She took Mae quite often since the park seemed to cheer her up and still fit in with her childlike moods.

At one point, Mae was getting on a ride and she told the young ride attendant, "We always go to the other Disneyland."

"The one in Orlando?" the attendant asked pertly.

"Disneyworld?

"No, the Disneyland in Anaheim," Mae said firmly.

"But this *is* Anaheim." The girl seemed puzzled.

"No!" Mae said indignantly. "The *other* Anaheim."

"I need a break," the girl said weakly as Emily laughed.

There was also the time when Emily took Mae to a local aquarium to walk around and see the fish. When they got home, Mae snuck out of the house and walked over to visit the neighbor next door. The neighbor called Emily and told her Mae was there.

"I hear you had a busy day." She laughed. "Mae told me you drove her to Russia!"

Emily just laughed until her ribs hurt.

Another time Mae thought her fiancé, Pete, would arrive home from Hawaii where he was stationed during World War II. He'd get home any day now, and they planned to go to Las Vegas to get married. These days tore Emily up inside because there was little she could do to comfort or reassure Mae. Nothing she could find to bring her back to the present. On these days, taking Mae out either to the amusement park, shopping, or to a movie seemed to cheer her up but only a little.

For Emily though, the movies turned into a strange double feature. Emily saw one movie, and then listened patiently as Mae described the movie she saw.

After one popular space movie Mae said loudly, "I really thought those were the most beautiful horses, didn't you?"

"I didn't see any horses, Mom," Emily muttered.

"You were probably too busy watching the sex scenes," Mae said with a trace of bitterness in her tone.

"There weren't any sex scenes, Mom." Emily pointed out, "It was a movie aimed at all ages, even kids."

"No sex scenes?" Mae exclaimed indignantly. "Then why did we even go?"

Emily laughed in spite of herself, but a part of her wondered if she had just gotten a small glimpse of a part of her mother's nature that she had not known about. She had always known her mother and father had a close relationship, but this one remark seemed to hint at a lusty nature that she had never associated with her mom.

Added to the stress was the joyful but stressful move out to David's house, and the job of dealing with her father's will and estate. She knew David was buried in his own legal practice, so she told him she would have the attorney who had drawn up the will handle the estate, although he did help her as much as he could. Her friends Kate, Laura and Lanie helped her with the move, along with their kids and husbands.

David was by her side as often as he could during this stressful period, but he was in the middle of several very serious negotiations, some of which he had already pushed back to help Emily. Now, to catch up, there were days and even evenings that he had to work. He managed to get home and eat dinner with Emily, Julia and Mae almost every night, except for a few days when he had to go out of town.

Kate and Laura came by as often as they could, sometimes bringing their husbands and kids. In spite of Mae's condition she was always good around the kids. Nicole came over, usually alone, but sometimes bringing a date. One of the dates she brought was David's law partner; the wedding was having a side effect, it seemed.

David took Emily out whenever he could, almost as if they were still dating. There were romantic dinners in the finest restaurants and quick meals from the drive-thru. They played pool and went to the movies, and also went riding, dancing, and swimming. Those dates were the brightest spots in Emily's world.

Her fitness program seemed to be stalled temporarily as the stress and grief of her father's loss made it harder for her to get motivated to workout. The added stress also increased her hunger and caused her to crave comfort foods, so sweets and breads went back on her menu and her weight began to go up. It wasn't a big gain, but it was noticeable and her new clothes started getting too tight. As a result, some of her old clothes came out of the closet. She started to feel sluggish, just not quite right. Even her monthly cycle became irregular.

With Nicole's help and prodding Emily kept working out, and slowly she began to feel like herself again. She even managed to control her hunger most of the time. She still never weighed herself, but Nicole measured her every four weeks. Nicole never told Emily what her measurements were, just how much she had lost or gained in her bust, waist, hips, and thighs.

One night, about six weeks later, David and Emily went out to dinner. After they ate they went home but they weren't ready to just go in and watch TV. The evening was warm and the moon was full. Emily went onto the house and pulled on a pair of shorts and they took the horses out on a moonlit trail ride. They stopped several times along the way to kiss each other, leaning from one horse to another.

"Emily, remember what you wanted to try doing on horseback?" David prodded, only half teasing. "Well, I had a fantasy. . ."

"What was it?" Emily was curious, her voice dropped to a velvet purr. "Tell me about it big guy."

"Well, we were riding just about here, at just about this time of the evening and I reminded you of your fantasy of making love on a horse."

"What did I do?"

"You blushed and looked around at the area we were riding in. I think you wanted to make sure we were well away from any houses or roads. I think you were wondering if you dared to do it. Then your silent decision was made and you removed your T-shirt without a word and tossed it on a fence post."

"Yeah, that's gonna happen." She laughed. "Not."

"Then while I watched in silent appreciation, you followed up it by removing your bra."

Emily snorted, there was no other word for it.

"Before I was so rudely interrupted," David laughed, "you managed to get Raider close enough to Target to reach over and unbutton my shirt. Then as I pulled it off you turned and loped Raider off, and I followed until we were back on my property."

"I was stunned by your actions, and I stopped to gather your shirt and bra before following you back to the ranch. I found you standing by the small arena. You had pulled Raider's bridle off and turned him loose. As I rode up, you met my eyes and stepped out of your shorts and panties in one quick motion. I swear, even in a fantasy, my heart stopped."

"Then it went like this . . ." David continued with a wolfish grin. "You looked up at me with a challenge in your eyes and asked, 'Aren't you going to get undressed?'"

"I said, 'On Target? Are you serious?' I was astonished."

"And you said 'Well on Target, in the barn, in the hot tub, what the heck,' you just grinned, 'We could even do it in bed.'"

"'Or all of the above?' I suggested."

"'Or all of the above.' You agreed."

"So I slid off my horse and gave you a leg up on him. I walked over, opened the arena gate, and stood there while you rode Target into the arena. You sat on the big horse and watched as I got undressed. I swung up behind you, and you put Target into his soft floating walk. I put my arms around you and gently teased your gorgeous full breasts. Pushing your hair aside, I nibbled on the back of your neck. Soon one of my hands lowered and began to tease your soft curls as you leaned back and savored the feel of my hardness behind you."

"With my support, you swung your right leg up on Target's neck so that you were riding sidesaddle, but bareback. With my help you managed to turn so that you were completely backwards on the horse, facing me. You slid your arms around my neck, kissing me. Your legs were on top of mine and we were very close, indeed, to making love when we both realized something."

David paused. Dramatically.

"What?" Emily demanded, aroused more than she wanted to admit. "Tell me!"

"Well," he paused, "we realized that the position we were in was really, I mean really uncomfortable."

"In fact you asked me 'How can I be so aroused and so uncomfortable at the same time?' as you moaned and leaned your head against my chest."

While David had been telling her this story, they had ridden home, reaching the barn.

"What followed was the best." David paused.

"I'll bite, what happened next?" Emily asked with a grin.

"I said, 'Well, you can't say we didn't give it a try. Why don't we adjourn to the barn?' And that's what we did in my fantasy," he finished.

"Did we now?" Emily mused. "And isn't it lucky that we're at the barn right now?"

"Sure is," David grinned. "Wanna get naked and take advantage of me?"

"I sure do."

They went into the barn and put a heavy clean horse blanket and a stall filled with fresh straw to good use. Eventually they wound up in the hot tub. They made love again, gently and passionately in the bubbling water.

Chapter Twenty

After they went into the house Emily took a quick shower and pulled on one of David's soft terrycloth robes. While she was getting ready David had opened a bottle of wine and started a fire. While he showered, Emily put some cheese and fruit on a plate. Together, they sat quietly in the den in front of the fire.

"Emily," David cuddled her in his arms while nibbling on her ear.

She turned and looked into his eyes. "What's up?"

"You know I love you, and I know you love me." She nodded silently, her eyes never leaving his. "There are so many things I love about you. You are so sweet and gentle. You are also sexy and uninhibited. I feel like you belong in my life. I even remember that when I first saw how caring you were with your parents, I realized you would be a wonderful wife and someday a wonderful mother."

"David," she turned in his arms and kissed him, "I can't imagine life without you."

Suddenly she broke off the kiss. "Mother?"

"Don't you want children?" David asked curiously.

"I'm not sure," Emily answered, thinking. "I mean in the future, of course, but I don't think I want to start a family just yet. In a way, I feel I have enough to take care of now. It's true my load has lifted a bit," she sniffed, "without Daddy to take care of, but I still miss him, and I'm still dealing with mother, and moving here. I'm even still dealing with being a wife, a very happy wife, but it's still all so new."

She gulped her wine then said, "People don't always realize it but even good changes can be stressful."

David gently stroked her shoulder and said, "I know."

She leaned into his arms. "Somehow, I just can't think of being responsible for another person right now. I mean, you're a grown man and you take care of yourself and you're still there for me, but a baby is so. . . Dependent, so helpless. I have to think it over, and we'll talk about it again. That is, of course, if we still have a choice. I've sometimes been careless with my protection, and I've been pretty irregular lately."

"That's probably just the stress from losing your father." David held her gently but he was a little hurt by Emily's reaction to the thought of having his kids.

"What if it's not?" she asked with a trace of panic. "What if I am pregnant already?"

"Then I'd be overjoyed," he told her grinning, then poked at her with his elbow. "But if you aren't, well, we can work on changing that."

She thought a minute, smiling to herself. "I know I'd be ecstatic once I got used to the idea. But as far as planning to get pregnant, I think I want to postpone that for a little while if it's okay with you. Anyway, I'll leave it in God's hands."

"He's done a great job for us so far, and besides, we're in this together." David was relaxed again, realizing that her slight hesitation was not because she didn't want his children.

The next day Emily wasn't feeling well. Her head was swimming as she stood up and she felt nauseous. The feeling passed fairly soon, but remembering the conversation from the night before all too clearly, she waited until she felt better and then drove into town to buy a home pregnancy test. She took the test as soon as she got home. It was negative. She wasn't sure if she was relieved or disappointed. Relief won out, by a narrow margin.

For the next few days she felt queasy off and on, but overall things were fine. She never mentioned the feelings to David. It wasn't always in the morning, but just a general unease that came at odd times. She worked out and felt fine most of the time, but she couldn't lose the few pounds she had gained.

She rode and swam every day. She learned to drive the horse trailer and took Raider over to Frank and Lanie's house to ride with their daughter. Cassie had recently turned 10, and she had an older horse that she rode in Western Equitation. Her trainer worked with Cassie and Emily, teaching them to look perfect on a horse, but the events bored Emily until the trainer started to work some new things. She began teaching Cassie and Emily how to ride in a trail horse event. Trail consisted of an obstacle course, walking over logs, backing between objects, walking over a rickety bridge, and through water, sometimes even a small jump, all of this was followed by railwork at a walk, jog, and canter. There was no set pattern, every event was different with course designs only limited by the course designer's imagination. Emily enjoyed the trail event, and Raider seemed to have a talent for it.

The other event she learned to enjoy was stock horse, which was run faster than most western equitation events. It consisted of cantering figure eights, running the length of the arena and sliding to a stop, and putting the horse into a spin, usually a full turn and a half.

Cassie was a lively, fun girl with a great sense of humor. She was becoming one of the best equitation riders in her age group. Going to work with her trainer gave Emily a chance to get to know Cassie and her folks, Frank and Lanie, a lot better. It also gave her a wider knowledge of horses and horse show events. She decided to talk to David about showing Raider in stock and trail.

Aside from all that, she went into the gym four times a week and did both cardio and strength workouts.

During that time, she did a few photo shoots. Then she started working in the gym, helping new members get started. Nikki believed that having a plus-sized girl working in the gym might make it less intimidating for some of the heavier girls to join. So many gyms had staff that all had perfect bodies. Nick wanted everyone represented on her staff. She also encouraged everyone to take photos regularly and keep an album to track their progress.

Emily also started thinking about going back to college and finishing her degree in Business Administration. She decided to try for the next spring term. She wasn't feeling sick exactly but she felt, well, off. And she was moody. Hopefully she'd feel better by spring.

Slowly she began to feel better. She rode in a few horse shows and was doing really well with Raider. Since most of the shows had all the events in one arena, with the Western equitation classes in the morning and the gymkhana in the afternoon, she even rode in a stock and trail and began to do fairly well, usually placing in the ribbons. She even won the trail class a few times.

A few months later, David asked her if she wanted to go with him to another overnight show, this time in Lancaster. She was eager to go. David managed to find a class in Trail that she could enter without conflicting with the gymkhana classes.

As the day to leave for the show approached, Emily's back began to ache. It was a sharp pain that came and went. She helped David load the trailer and rode with him to the show grounds without telling him about her backache. She wondered to herself if she had lifted something too heavy, or done it the wrong way. They got to the show grounds, unloaded the trailer and set up their stalls, putting the straw and feed in for the horses, hanging up tack and arranging equipment.

They went to dinner and then checked into the hotel. Once she got to the hotel she felt much better. They made tender love, and fell asleep in each other's arms.

The next day she got up with David and went to the show grounds with him to feed the horses and clean out the stalls. After the horses finished eating, they groomed them to a glossy shine and saddled them up. They headed for the warm up arena, each working their horse slowly, walking and jogging until the horses were warmed up and limber.

She took Raider through some rollbacks along the fence line of the warm-up arena. She was nervous because she had to ride in the senior event. She no longer qualified for novice. She knew she'd have to ride much better to win any ribbons at all.

The show started and the first event was Keyhole. She had a good ride, but her time was too slow for a ribbon. She managed to place 4th in Single pole and 3rd in Pole bending. She concentrated and had a great ride in Quadrangle and earned a 2nd. Between events, she rested, trying to ignore the growing backache and an increasing abdominal pain. But during speed barrels Raider slipped and fell. It was her first fall and Emily lay in the dirt, feeling thousands of aches and pains, but she managed to stand up as she saw David running towards her, his face white with fear. She managed to calm him down and reassure him that she wasn't injured, but she felt stiff. She got on and tried to ride Raider around but she was too stiff. Her backache was getting worse, too. After the fall, she told David she'd have to scratch from the afternoon events.

One of the other riders, a nurse named Anna, sat down and talked to her during a break in the action, shooing David out to check on Raider's legs and take care of him.

She finished with, "I'm sure most of your aches and pains are from the fall. You're lucky not to have any scrapes or cuts. I'd keep that leg up and keep some ice on it. Also, if I didn't know better, I'd say you were pregnant."

"I took a home pregnancy test several months back," Emily admitted. "My periods had been very irregular, and I had gained about fifteen pounds. But the test came back negative."

"Still, have you had any unprotected sex in the last nine months?" she persisted.

"Well, yes, lots of times, but even if the test was wrong, I have an RN living with me. Wouldn't she notice?" Emily paced uncomfortably.

"Maybe not, you sure don't have a pregnancy belly." She smiled. "Is it getting worse?"

She peered into Emily's eyes.

"Yes." Emily nodded.

Just then, David came into the tack room. "How is she?"

"I'm sure she's find, she just needs to keep ice on her leg," the nurse said. Then she casually asked, "David, will you do me a favor and scratch me from the rest of the day's events? And please ask the ambulance attendants to come and check Emily out?"

"I thought they looked at her at the arena." He was worried and trying not to let it show.

"They did, I just think a quick follow-up may be in order." She smiled calmly at David. "Did Emily tell you she wasn't feeling very well before the fall?"

"No, she said she was fine." David reached out to take Emily's hand. "But I had a feeling. . . I'll be back."

He kissed Emily and left in a hurry.

"I have an idea," Anna said calmly. "Why don't we get you out of those jeans and into something more comfortable?"

The only thing she could find was one of David's shirts. It had long tails that came down Emily's legs. Anna helped Emily change and as she worked she asked, "Why don't you lay down again until we get the paramedics here to check you out? Can't hurt."

Anna helped Emily lie on the cot they'd put in the tack room. She spread a light horse blanket over her legs.

She asked Emily softly, "Can I take a quick look?"

At Emily's nod she followed the question with action by raising the blanket and taking a quick look.

"Emily, I'm afraid you're wrong about not being pregnant," she said with a smile. "You're in active labor and almost fully dilated."

"How can I be?" Emily gasped. "I rode in a horse show today!"

"Yeah, both of you did." She laughed. "And you did really well."

"Until I fell." Emily worried. "Anna, do you think the fall hurt my baby?"

"I'm not sure, that's why I wanted the paramedics on hand, but I think the way you landed, on your backside, was the best way to land. I'm sure the baby is fine."

Just then Emily's water broke.

"But I haven't had any labor pains, just a backache!" Emily protested. "And a general sense of not being well."

"Consider yourself lucky." She held Emily's hand. "I felt like I'd swallowed a turkey for months, and then had nineteen hours of labor."

"I guess I am lucky," Emily gasped, finally feeling a contraction, "but surprised. I watched this TV show about women who gave birth without ever knowing they were pregnant, do you know the one I mean?"

Anna nodded and Emily continued, "I thought those women were really dumb. Now, I'm one of them."

"And you're not dumb."

The paramedics came hurrying in, followed by David. The nurse told them Emily was too far along to be moved. In fact, she was fully dilated and crowning.

"Okay, Ma'am, on your next contraction give a push," the paramedic said.

"Our baby's going to be born in a barn," Emily said. "That can't be good."

"Sweetheart, it was good enough for Christ." David could hardly stop smiling.

And it worked out just fine for Emily, too.

After the baby boy was born, they bundled Emily and the baby up and transported them to the hospital.

"We need a name for him," David said as he leaned over and kissed Emily gently. "How about Pete?"

"Daddy would love that, and David for a middle name?"

"Works for me."

At the hospital they whisked Emily and the baby away to check them both out. David filled out the endless forms and then finally got on his cell phone and called Nick, who said she'd fly home immediately. Next he called Kate and told her.

For once she was stunned speechless. When she got over her shock, she said she'd call the 'gang' and they'd set up a nursery for the baby.

Kate got into action; she enlisted her friends Laura, Lanie, and their husbands, plus talked to Julia and had her take care of Mae. Her husband drove her to the hardware store where she picked out a paint color and a paint that was especially made to be odorless and safe for newborns. Then they went to the house and met with Laura and Lanie. The husbands got to work painting the bedroom next to the master bedroom and the women went shopping.

"Hey!" The men protested, "How come you get the fun part and we get the hard part?"

"Because we get the hard part of the pregnancy, and as for hard parts, it's yours that causes all the problems, anyway." Kate laughed at them.

The women went to a store that specialized in baby things and went nuts. They got it all: the crib, changing table, a rocking chair, tons of cute clothes, onesies, rattles, pacifiers and more. And diapers, lots and lots of diapers. They had just about finished the room when Nick arrived.

David called and said they'd be home the next day.

Shortly after they got home, David was sitting next to Emily watching her nurse the baby.

"Emily, do you know what tomorrow is?" he asked.

She thought. "No, what is it?"

"It's the anniversary of the day we met."

"Oh my goodness!" Emily gasped. "Who could have believed a year ago that the day I volunteered at a horse show would be the day that changed my life?"

"Yeah, a year ago you said you were dreaming of tomorrow, well tomorrow's here. Did it live up to your dreams?"

"God's been very good to me and gave me more than I could ever dream of, so much more." Emily smiled as she leaned in to kiss her husband.

Epilogue

When Kate, Laura and Lanie came to visit, once they had seen and coddled the baby, they sat in Emily's living room drinking orange juice.

Laura remarked, "Wow! Emily, you met the perfect man and you never had to go hunting for him. You just kind of ran into him."

Lanie paced and turned to face Emily. "You also never had to lift a hand for your wedding!"

Kate gulped her juice. "And you never had to suffer the symptoms of pregnancy: the morning sickness, the mood swings, feeling like you swallowed a blimp, or even labor pains. What *did* you do for all this?"

Emily laughed, then winked at them. "I prayed."

Other books by Susan Kohler

The Paddle Club

Hot Crossed Buns

Another Batch of Warm Buns

The Heart of The Beast

Working Romance

Who's Taming Who?

Asentaderas Cruzadas Calientes
(Spanish language edition of *Hot Crossed Buns*)

Note to Readers

Please visit my website at:

www.susankohlernovels.com

I have excerpts and information on my novels: the kinky ones, the dark historical romance, and the contemporary romances.

Sue

www.ingramcontent.com/pod-product-compliance
Lightning Source LLC
Chambersburg PA
CBHW020334260626
47156CB00004B/1519